German essayist, cultural critic, and novelist, THOMAS MANN was awarded the Nobel Prize in Literature in 1929. Among his most famous works are *Buddenbrooks*, published when he was just twenty-six, *The Magic Mountain*, and *Doctor Faustus*.

Translator MICHAEL HENRY HEIM is a professor of Slavic languages and literature at UCLA. A graduate of Columbia College and Harvard University, his many translations include Chekhov's *The Seagull*, *Uncle Vanya*, *Three Sisters*, and *The Cherry Orchard*, as well as Milan Kundera's *The Book of Laughter and Forgetting* and *The Unbearable Lightness of Being*.

Death in Venice

THOMAS MANN

Translated by
MICHAEL HENRY HEIM

Introduction by
MICHAEL CUNNINGHAM

ecco

An Imprint of HarperCollinsPublishers

First Ecco paperback edition published June 2005

Designed by Claire Naylon Vaccaro

The Library of Congress has catalogued the hardcover edition as follows:

Mann, Thomas, 1875–1955.
[Tod in Venedig. English]
Death in Venice / by Thomas Mann; [translated by Michael Henry Heim].
p. cm.
ISBN 0-06-057605-7 (alk. paper)
I. Heim, Michael Henry. II. Title.
PT2625.A44T62 2004
833′.912—dc22   2003063111

ISBN 978-0-06-057617-2 (pbk.)

05 06 07 08 09 ❖/RRD 10 9 8 7 6 5 4 3 2 1

Introduction

MICHAEL CUNNINGHAM

All novels are translations, even in their original languages. This has been revealed to me over time, as I've worked with the various dedicated (and inevitably underpaid) people who have agreed to translate my own books. When I started working with translators, I couldn't help noticing that many of the problems that vexed them—questions of nuance, resonance, and tone, as well as the rhythms of the sentences themselves—were familiar to me. I'd worried over the same things when I wrote the book in the first place. It dawned on me, gradually, that I was a translator, too. I had taken the raw material of the book in question and translated it into language.

Every writer of course works differently, but I suspect that most novels begin in their writers' minds as confusions of images, impulses, scattered meanings, devotions, grudges, fixations, and some vague sort of plot, to name just a few. A novel in its earliest form, before it begins to be rendered into language, is a cloud of sorts that hovers over the writer's head, a mystery born with clues to its own meanings but also, at its heart, insoluble. One hopes—a novel is inevitably an expression of unreasonable hopes—that the finished book will contain not only characters and scenes but a certain larger truth, though that truth, whatever it may be, is impossible to express fully in words. It has to do with the fact that writer and reader both know, beneath the level of active consciousness, something about being alive and being mortal, and that that something, when we try to express it, inevitably eludes us. We are creatures whose innate knowledge exceeds that which can be articulated. Although language is enormously powerful, it is concrete, and so it can't help but miniaturize, to a certain extent, that which we simply *know*. All the writers I respect want to write a book so penetrating and thorough, so compassionate and unrelenting, that it can stand unembarrassed beside the spectacle of life itself. And all writers I respect seem to know (though no one likes to talk about it) that our efforts are doomed from the outset. Life is bigger than literature. We do the best we can. Some of us do better than others.

My own translators, the best ones, seem always to

battle a sense of failure—the conviction that while they've come close they've missed something in the original, some completeness, some aliveness, that refuses to quite come through in French or Italian or Japanese. This, too, is familiar to me. I always feel the same when a novel has finally exhausted me, and I feel compelled to admit that, although it doesn't seem finished, it is as close to completion as I'm capable of getting it. Some wholeness isn't quite there. While I wrote, I felt it hovering around me. I could taste it, I could almost *smell* it— the mystery itself. And even if the published novel has turned out fairly well, there is always that sense of having missed the mark.

Fiction is, then, at least to me, an ongoing process of translation (and mistranslation), beginning with the writer's earliest impulses and continuing through its rendering into Icelandic or Korean or Catalan. Writers and translators are engaged in the same effort, at different stages along the line.

For a handful of the greatest writers, Thomas Mann among them, the process of translation continues even further. Occasionally a book like *Death in Venice* speaks so enduringly to readers that it is translated not once but again, and sometimes again and again. This is as it should be. It respects the fundamental nature of literature as a

mutable and ever-unresolved business involving writers'
and readers' ongoing attempts to get to the heart of the
matter, to complete that which can never be completed. A
great book is probably, by definition, too complex and lay-
ered, too intricately alive, to be translated once and for all.

Michael Henry Heim's new translation of *Death in
Venice* subtly but clearly extends and alters previous translations. What we have here is the same book, and a new
book. Before I talk about the particulars of Heim's translation, though, I should briefly mention something else
I've learned by working with translators. Good translators
(and here they differ from the writers of the original text)
agonize over a fundamental question. To what extent
should they render, to the best of their ability, the words
as written, and to what extent should they reinterpret
them to suit the particulars of the language and culture
into which they are being conveyed? Every language has
its own cadences; a sentence that snaps and sparkles in
one language is likely to go flat if conveyed slavishly, word
by word, into another. How much license, then, should a
translator take in rewriting the sentences so that their
music, the pure *sound* of them, comes through? And how, if
at all, should the translator accommodate the fact that
certain images and phrases, and even some basic vocabulary, resonate differently from culture to culture? Russian

contains no term for "privacy," at least not in the Anglo-American sense of privacy as a desirable and even necessary refuge. To the Chinese, the fact that a man is wearing a Bill Blass suit means nothing at all, while to an American (well, to some Americans) it implies a good deal about the man's outmoded, rather clueless sense of style.

Reading Heim's translation, I was struck by a fine but pervasive difference between it and the *Death in Venice* I remembered. It goes without saying that the basic events are the same. In both versions Gustav von Aschenbach, a celebrated German author who finds himself, as Dante put it, "In the middle of the journey of [his] life . . . in a dark wood, where the right road had been lost sight of" (from Seamus Heaney's 1993 translation), goes on a holiday in hope of reviving his fading enthusiasm for life. He travels to Venice, where he becomes first enamored of and then obsessed by a fourteen-year-old Polish boy named Tadzio, who is, in fleshly form, the very ideal of youthful human beauty, with all youth and beauty can imply to the no-longer-young about yearning, mortality, and the extravagant carelessness of a god who gives us life and then, by slow degrees, takes it back again. Aschenbach is increasingly consumed by his passion, until he dies on the beach at the Lido, done up in a grotesque parody of youth, rouged and lipsticked, watching Tadzio from afar.

And yet, the tone of Aschenbach's decline felt different in Heim's version. I remembered Aschenbach as a figure of pure pathos. I'd always thought that Mann was telling us, in part (a great writer is always telling us many things at once, some of them contradictory), that if we aren't careful, we, too, could end up dying alone on a beach, our love unrequited, wearing too much jewelry, our hair unnaturally black. In that regard, Aschenbach has long been a perversely mythic figure to me. As I approach the age at which Aschenbach expired I've fallen into the habit of asking, every now and then, when I'm uncertain about a sartorial gesture, whether the scarf or ruffle in question makes me look a bit *Death in Venice*-ish.

Although the Aschenbach of Heim's translation ends up every bit as gaudily dressed and made up, and every bit as alone, he felt to me this time less clownish and more tragic; more like a man whose desperation and delusion are not only sad but also heroic. This time around, Mann seemed to be saying that yes, we all fade, we're all going to the same place, and so we might as well go down in a blaze of love, however we may degrade ourselves in the process, however ill-advised our taste in clothes and makeup. This Aschenbach felt larger, and at least a little bit more profound. This Mann seemed to say, via Aschenbach, that if the alternative is to age gracefully, to gray and wither quietly, untroubled by absurd or perverse passions—if the other option is to shuffle offstage without attracting undue notice—it might in fact be better to do ourselves up like dandies, to discard our precious dignity, to worship what we know we cannot have right up until the moment of our demise. If I say that this Aschenbach put me in mind of Divine in Jean Genet's *Our Lady of the Flowers*, I mean it as a tribute. In the Genet book, Divine, a drag queen of a certain age, is carrying on at a bar when his faux-pearl coronet breaks. The pearls scatter everywhere, and Divine's rival queens, exquisitely attuned to the faintest hint of blood in the water, proclaim him uncrowned, the Fallen One. Divine simply takes his dentures out and plunks them onto his head, declaring, "Dammit all, ladies, I'll be queen anyhow."* The Aschenbach of the Heim translation shares some of Divine's heedless heroism. All our coronets will break, sooner or later. When that happens it's probably best to just put our false teeth onto our heads, have a laugh, and continue. Aschenbach can hardly be said to have a laugh (it's hard to imagine a more humorless great writer than Mann), and he does not of course continue, but in this version he seems less a figure of pure sorrow and more a

* Jean Genet, *Our Lady of the Flowers* (New York: Grove Press, 1976), 193.

very distant relation to Divine. This version seems to suggest that Aschenbach may be doing the best he can—the best anyone can—with the whole business of decay; the fact that, since mortality always wins, we might as well go down in our full colors, wracked by longing, with our false teeth on our heads.

When I'd finished reading the Heim translation, I couldn't tell whether the difference resided in the new version or in my own mind. There is this, too, about the mutability of literature—the books we read at twenty are not the books we read at fifty, because we are not the same people. Figures like Huck Finn, Anna Karenina, and Emma Bovary are likely to seem very different to us at different points in our lives, though who they are and what they do changes not at all. I wondered if Aschenbach struck me as grander and braver simply because I am now more or less his age, and more subject than I once was to my own questions about whether or not a little strategically applied dye or rouge might help me feel more vital.

I compared Heim's version to the one I read in college, which was done by H. T. Lowe-Porter in 1930. There have been a couple of other attempts, made relatively recently, but Lowe-Porter's translation is the one with which most of us grew up—the definitive *Death in Venice* for those who can read English but not German. I'm relieved to say that, as far as I can tell, this altered Aschenbach is not merely a figment of my own aging imagination. Heim's *Death in Venice* is, generally, a more lyrical, sympathetic book—a slightly more intimate and personal book—than Lowe-Porter's rather stern, disapproving one. Lowe-Porter gave us a clownish, foolish Aschenbach—a figure who would not seem out of place in a Fellini movie. Heim also gives us a man in the throes of passion, and treats him with the respect that passion deserves.

A comparison like this summons up the mother of all questions regarding different translations of the same book: How can we possibly decide, unless we're fluent in both languages, which is more faithful to the author's intent? Readers who know English and German (I am not one of them) have long complained about certain inarguable mistakes in Lowe-Porter's translation. I assume Heim has corrected them. Still, a handful of blunders does not seem likely to alter the fundamental tone of a book, or seriously subvert its meaning. Any assertion that a translation can be rendered "accurate" if its blatant errors are corrected underestimates the art and magic of translation. A translation, any translation, is filtered through a particular sensibility, and so the discrepancies, as they accrue, must be, at least to some extent, an expression of whatever the translator brought to the job. However multilingual we may be as readers, we find ourselves faced with a fundamental, inescapable responsibility. We must understand that any book, and especially a great one, is a complex and highly personal exchange between its writer and its readers. None of us reads precisely the same book, even if the words are identical. Readers, too, are part of the ongoing process of translation, the one that originates in the author's mind. My *Death in Venice,* whichever translation I read, is slightly different from anyone else's. My Mann is, to a certain extent, my own private, personal Mann, as is everyone's. We agree about his basic qualities and intentions, but spin them according to our own natures. There is, in a sense, no definitive *Death in Venice.* We must, all of us, decide for ourselves what Mann meant to give us, and what we are willing to receive.

That said, a comparison of the two versions suggests that Mann in the original tends toward a Wagnerian stateliness that is generally magisterial and elevating but also, occasionally, rather rigid and chill. There is the sporadic feeling that in writing this particular tale of doomed love, Mann comes off a bit like a giant trying to manage a porcelain tea set. He laid a heavy hand upon the world. He never intended to dart around like a dragonfly. He was, in all his work, *Herr Professor*, every bit as august and severe as Aschenbach himself, and his language reflects his nature. He was, in a certain sense, among the last of his kind. Although he was a contemporary of writers like Virginia Woolf and James Joyce, he was distinctly a member of the previous generation. Woolf, Joyce, and others would change not only the form of the novel but the relationship between novelist and reader. The novelists of the later twentieth century would, by and large, do away with the whole notion of lofty authority, and offer in its place a kind of egalitarianism. The novelist would be less the distinguished lecturer and more the fellow student; he or she would be more determined to write about everyday life and to say, in essence, to readers, Here it all is, here are its mythic resonances, here are its smells and tastes, *you* tell *me* what it means. Mann's sense of moral responsibility, and the stentorian prose appropriate to such a sense, would be shrugged off by those who came after him. Language itself, in fiction, would become a more fluid and vital part of the whole. We would, for the most part, dispense with the notion of the author as architect, carving sentences out of granite and setting them one atop another in support of a great theme. We revere the novels of Eliot, Dickens, Hardy, and others, but we do not remember and cherish individual lines, not the way we do lines from Joyce or Woolf. We aren't meant to. After Mann, language would receive a promotion. Sentences would be musical and meaningful in and of themselves. They would not be asked to serve primarily as columns or pedestals. They would be encouraged to draw a certain degree of attention to themselves.

We can probably tell a good deal about an era by its most prominent literary characters. The twentieth century gave us Leopold Bloom, Clarissa Dalloway, Humbert Humbert, and Jay Gatsby, among others, and it gave us Gustav von Aschenbach. They are, on one hand, a rather motley crew. Here is Mrs. Dalloway buying flowers. Here is Gatsby staring at the green light on Daisy Buchanan's dock. And here is Aschenbach, our Icarus, flying too high, melting, and crashing down on a beach. For all their differences, though, these characters have a certain commonality. They are, all of them, small figures in an immense landscape. They are all undernourished, though the world has given them everything they need to survive, at least in terms of food and shelter. They are all on quests, and if the objects of their desire seem rather modest—one wants to give a perfect party, another wants his childhood sweetheart back—it is the very modesty of those wishes, conjoined with their unattainability, that breaks our hearts. Most of the heroes of twentieth-century European and American literature are striving not against marital constraints or humble origins or political systems, but against loss itself. Some of them end up better than others, but none of them wins.

Aschenbach is, to me at least, the most devastating of the lot. Like any enduring literary figure, he is both of his time and beyond it. He is descended from King Lear, the most glorious of all misguided spirits, though before Heim's translation we might not fully have understood that. By fine-tuning certain details, by reconsidering word choices, Heim's translation achieves a startling effect. It rescues Aschenbach from the realm of the cautionary and places him where he belongs, in the pantheon of fictive men and women whose impossible yearnings make them as deeply human as characters can be. It's a dark gift, what Heim has given us. Here we have an Aschenbach who is harder to dismiss, whose fate is larger and nobler, if not exactly more comforting. Here is an Aschenbach who is more clearly and unavoidably all of us, who wants more than life is willing to provide, whose defeat is so bound up with his heroism that the two can't be easily separated. That may or may not be exactly what Mann had in mind. There's no way of knowing. But it is, for my purposes at least, the grander and more humane book that Mann meant to give us all along.

One

Gustav Aschenbach or von Aschenbach, as he had officially been known since his fiftieth birthday, set out alone from his residence in Munich's Prinzregentenstrasse on a spring afternoon in 19..—a year that for months had shown so ominous a countenance to our continent—with the intention of taking an extended walk. Overwrought from the difficult and dangerous labors of the late morning hours, labors demanding the utmost caution, prudence, tenacity, and precision of will, the writer had even after the midday meal been unable to halt the momentum of the inner mechanism—the *motus animi continuus* in which, according to Cicero, eloquence resides—and find the refreshing sleep that the growing wear and tear upon his forces had made a daily necessity. And so, shortly after tea he had sought the outdoors in the hope that open air and exercise might revive him and help him to enjoy a fruitful evening.

It was early May, and after a few cold, wet weeks a mock summer had set in. The Englischer Garten, though as yet in tender bud, was as muggy as in August and full of vehicles and pedestrians on the city side. At Aumeister, to which he had been led by ever more solitary paths, Aschenbach briefly scanned the crowded and lively open-air restaurant and the cabs and carriages along its edge, then, the sun beginning to sink, headed home across the open fields beyond the park, but feeling tired and noticing a storm brewing over Föhring, he stopped at the Northern Cemetery to wait for the tram that would take him straight back to town.

As it happened, there was no one at the tram stop or thereabouts. Nor was any vehicle to be seen on the paved roadway of the Ungererstrasse—whose gleaming tracks stretched solitary in the direction of Schwabing—or on the road to Föhring. There was nothing stirring behind the stonemasons' fences, where crosses, headstones, and monuments for sale formed a second, uninhabited grave-yard, and the mortuary's Byzantine structure opposite stood silent in the glow of the waning day. Its façade, decorated with Greek crosses and brightly hued hieratic patterns, also displayed a selection of symmetrically arranged gilt-lettered inscriptions concerning the after-life, such as "They Enter into the Dwelling Place of the Lord" or "May the Light Everlasting Shine upon Them," and reading the formulas, letting his mind's eye lose itself in the mysticism emanating from them, served to distract the waiting man for several minutes until, resurfacing from his reveries, he noticed a figure in the portico above the two apocalyptic beasts guarding the staircase, and something slightly out of the ordinary in the figure's appearance gave his thoughts an entirely new turn.

Whether the man had emerged from the chapel's inner sanctum through the bronze gate or mounted the steps unobtrusively from outside was uncertain. Without giving the matter much thought, Aschenbach inclined towards the first hypothesis. The man—of medium height, thin, beardless, and strikingly snub-nosed—was the red-haired type and had its milky, freckled pigmentation. He was clearly not of Bavarian stock and, if nothing else, the broad, straight-brimmed bast hat covering his head lent him a distinctly foreign, exotic air. He did, however, have the customary knapsack strapped to his shoulders, wore a yellowish belted suit of what appeared to be loden, and carried a gray waterproof over his left forearm, which he pressed to his side, and an iron-tipped walking stick in his right hand, and having thrust the stick diagonally into the ground, he had crossed his feet and braced one hip on its crook. Holding his head high and thus exposing a strong, bare Adam's apple on the thin neck rising out of his loose, open shirt, he gazed alert into the distance with colorless, red-lashed eyes, the two pronounced vertical furrows between them oddly suited to the short, turned-up nose. Thus—and perhaps his elevated and elevating position contributed to the impression—there was something of the overseer, something lordly, bold, even wild in his demeanor, for be it that he was grimacing, blinded by the setting sun, or that he had a permanent facial deformity, his lips seemed too short:

they pulled all the way back, baring his long, white teeth to the gums.

Aschenbach's half-distracted, half-inquisitive scrutiny of the stranger may have been lacking in discretion, for he suddenly perceived that the man was returning his stare and was indeed so belligerently, so directly, so blatantly determined to challenge him publicly and force him to withdraw it that Aschenbach, embarrassed, turned away and set off along the fence, vaguely resolved to take no further notice of him. A minute later he had forgotten the man. It may have been the stranger's perambulatory appearance that acted upon his imagination or some other physical or psychological influence coming into play, but much to his surprise he grew aware of a strange expansion of his inner being, a kind of restive anxiety, a fervent youthful craving for faraway places, a feeling so vivid, so new or else so long outgrown and forgotten that he came to a standstill and—hands behind his back, eyes on the ground, rooted to the spot—examined the nature and purport of the feeling.

It was wanderlust, pure and simple, yet it had come

upon him like a seizure and grown into a passion—no, more, an hallucination. His desire sprouted eyes, his imagination, as yet unstilled from its morning labors, conjured forth the earth's manifold wonders and horrors in his attempt to visualize them: he saw. He saw a landscape, a tropical quagmire beneath a steamy sky—sultry, luxuriant, and monstrous—a kind of primordial wilderness of islands, marshes, and alluvial channels; saw hairy palm shafts thrusting upward, near and far, from rank clusters of bracken, from beds of thick, swollen, and bizarrely burgeoning flora; saw fantastically malformed trees plunge their roots through the air into the soil, into stagnant, shadow-green, looking-glass waters, where, amidst milk-white flowers bobbing like bowls, outlandish stoop-shouldered birds with misshapen beaks stood stock-still in the shallows, peering off to one side; saw the eyes of a crouching tiger gleam out of the knotty canes of a bamboo thicket—and felt his heart pound with terror and an enigmatic craving. Then the vision faded, and with a shake of the head Aschenbach resumed his promenade along the gravestone cutters' fences.

He had—at least since he could afford the advantages of traveling the world at will—regarded tourism as nothing but a hygienic precaution to be taken willy-nilly from time to time. Preoccupied with the tasks imposed upon him by his ego and the European psyche, overburdened by the obligation to produce, averse to diversion, and no lover of the external world and its variety, he was quite content with the view of the earth's surface that anyone can gain without stirring far from home, and never so much as tempted to venture beyond Europe. Especially now that his life was on the decline and his fear of failing to achieve his artistic goals—the concern that his time might run out before he had accomplished what he needed to accomplish and given fully of himself— could no longer be dismissed as a caprice, he had confined his external existence almost exclusively to the beautiful city that had become his home and the rustic cottage he had built for himself in the mountains and where he spent the rainy summers.

Thus it was that the sudden and belated impulse which had come over him was soon restrained and redressed by reason and the self-discipline he had practiced from an early age. He had intended to reach a certain point in his work, which was his life, before moving to the country, and the thought of leaving his desk for months to go gallivanting around the world seemed too frivolous and disruptive to be taken seriously. Yet he knew only too well the source of the sudden temptation. It was an urge to flee—he fully admitted it, this yearning for freedom, release, oblivion—an urge to flee his work, the humdrum routine of a rigid, cold, passionate duty. Granted, he loved that duty and even almost loved the enervating daily struggle between his proud, tenacious, much-tested will and the growing fatigue, which no one must suspect or the finished product betray by the slightest sign of foundering or neglect. But it made sense not to go too far in the other direction, not to be so obstinate as to curb a need erupting with such virulence. He thought of his work, of the point at which, yesterday and again today, he had had to abandon it since it had refused to yield to either patient attention or a swift bit of legerdemain. He had examined the passage anew, trying to shatter or diffuse his block, only to renounce the effort with a shudder of revulsion. There was no unwonted difficulty involved; no, he was paralyzed by the scruples arising from his distaste for the project, which made themselves felt in demands impossible to satisfy. Impossible demands had of course impressed the young man as the very essence and innermost nature of talent, and it was for them that he had bridled and cooled his feelings, knowing they are prone to make do with blithe approximations and half-perfections. Could it be that his indentured sensibility was now taking its revenge, abandoning him and refusing henceforth to bear his art on its wings, depriving him of all pleasure, all delight in form and expression? Not that he produced poor work: such at least was the advantage of his years that he felt serenely confident of his mastery. Yet, much as the nation might honor it, it gave him no pleasure: he felt it lacked those flights of fiery, playful fancy, the product of joy, which more than any intrinsic content—great merit that it might have—delight the discriminating public. He dreaded the summer in the country, all alone in the cottage with the maid who cooked his meals and the man who served them; he dreaded the sight of the familiar mountain peaks and slopes that would once more encompass his torpid discontent. He needed a change of scene, a bit of spontaneity, an idle existence, a foreign atmosphere, and an influx of new blood to make the summer bearable and productive. He *would* travel, then; good, he was satisfied. Not too far, not all the way to the tigers. A night in a sleeping car and a siesta of three or four weeks at one of the internationally recognized holiday resorts in the friendly south . . .

Such were his reflections as the clang of the electric tram reached him along the Ungererstrasse, and mounting the platform he decided to spend the evening studying maps and timetables. He thought of looking back to find the man in the bast hat, his companion during what had turned into a fateful wait, but he was unable to determine the man's whereabouts: he was neither at his previous location nor at the next stop nor in the tram.

Two

The author of a limpid and powerful prose epic dealing with the life of Frederick the Great; the patient artist who in his boundless diligence had woven a rich tapestry of a novel, *Maya* by name, that brings together myriad human fates in the service of an idea; the creator of a trenchant tale entitled "A Wretched Figure" that had earned him the gratitude of the younger generation by showing it a path to moral fortitude existing even beyond the depths of knowledge; and lastly (here ends the list of his mature works) the thinker whose impassioned treatise, "Art and the Intellect," had led serious critics to rank him, on the strength of the work's rigorous logic and eloquent use of antitheses, alongside Schiller and his meditation "On Naive and Sentimental Poetry"—Gustav Aschenbach was born in L., a county town in the province of Silesia, the son of a senior official in the judiciary. His forebears had been officers, judges, and civil servants, men who led disciplined, decently austere lives serving king and state. A certain inner spirituality had manifested itself in the person of the only clergyman amongst them, and a strain of more impetuous, sensual blood had found its way into the family in the previous generation through the writer's mother, the daughter of a Bohemian bandmaster. She was the source of the foreign racial features in his appearance. It was the union of the father's sober, conscientious nature with the darker, more fiery impulses of the mother that engendered the artist—and this particular artist.

Since his entire being was bent on fame, he proved himself if not quite precocious then at least, thanks to the resolute and precise persona he cultivated, mature and ready for life in the world before his time. Barely out of school he had acquired a name for himself. In the space of ten years he had learned to perform his professional duties and manage his fame from his writing desk and to make every sentence of his correspondence gracious and pregnant with meaning (letters had to be brief, because the demands made on the staunch and successful are many). The forty-year-old, worn down by the strains and vicissitudes of his work, had to cope with a daily mail bearing stamps from all over the world.

Equidistant from the banal and the eccentric, his talent seemed tailored to gain both the confidence of the general public and the demanding admiration of the connoisseur. Since boyhood he had been pressed from all sides to achieve—and to achieve the extraordinary—and thus had never known leisure, the carefree idleness of youth. When in about his thirty-fifth year he was taken ill in Vienna, an astute observer said of him in public, "Here is how Aschenbach has always lived"—and he made a tight fist of his left hand—"not like this"—and he let his open hand dangle freely from the arm of his chair. That rang true, and what made Aschenbach all the more heroic and noble was that he was not robust by nature, that he was merely called to constant industry, not born to it.

Medical concerns had kept the boy out of school and dependent on private tutoring. He had grown up solitary and friendless and must have realized early that he belonged to a species for which talent was less a rarity than physical strength—the strength needed to make something of the talent—a species that tended to make the most of its powers early, seldom developing them into old age. But his motto was *Durchhalten,* "Persevere," and he regarded his Frederick-the-Great novel as nothing short of the apotheosis of this command, which he considered the essence of a cardinal virtue: action in the face of suffering. Then, too, he ardently desired to live to old age, for he had always believed that the only artistic gift that can be called truly great, all-encompassing, and, yes, truly praiseworthy is one that has been vouchsafed productivity at all stages of human existence.

Wishing to bear on such frail shoulders the burdens imposed by his talent and wishing to go far, he had great need of discipline, and discipline was fortunately an inborn quality he had inherited from his father's side of the family. At forty, at fifty, and even when younger, at an age when others dissipate their talents, wax rhapsodic, or blissfully defer their grand projects, he would start his day early by dashing cold water over his chest and back; then, having set a pair of tall wax candles in silver holders at the head of his manuscript, he would spend two or three fervent, conscientious hours offering up to art the strength he had garnered in sleep. It was a forgivable error—indeed, it betokened a victory for his moral stance—that the uninitiated should take the world of his *Maya* or the epic background against which Frederick's feats unfolded as the product of prodigious strength and unending stamina, but in fact they grew out of daily increments of hundreds upon hundreds of bits of inspiration, and the only reason they were so perfect—overall and in every detail—was that their creator had held out for years under the strain of a single work with a fortitude and tenacity analogous to those Frederick had used to conquer his native province, and that he had devoted only his most vibrant and vital hours to its composition.

For a major product of the intellect to make an immediate broad and deep impact it must rest upon a secret affinity, indeed, a congruence between the personal destiny of its author and the collective destiny of his generation. The people do not know why they bestow fame upon a given work of art. Though far from connoisseurs, they believe they have discovered a hundred virtues to justify such enthusiasm, yet the true basis for their acclaim is an imponderable, mere affinity. Once, in a less than conspicuous passage, Aschenbach stated outright that nearly everything great owes its existence to "despites": despite misery and affliction, poverty, desolation, physical debility, vice, passion, and a thousand other obstacles. But it was more than an observation; it was his experience, the very formula of his life and fame, the key to his work. Was it any wonder, therefore, that it likewise informed the moral makeup and external demeanor of his most representative protagonists?

The new type of hero that he favored and that recurred in a variety of forms had been analyzed quite early by a shrewd critic, who said it rested on "an intellectual, adolescent conception of manliness," one that "stands by calmly, gritting its teeth in proud shame, while swords and spears pierce its flesh." It was all very beautiful, clever, and precise, though it erred on the side of passivity. Because composure in the face of destiny and equanimity in the face of torture are not mere matters of endurance; they are an active achievement, a positive triumph, and the Sebastian figure is the most beautiful symbol if not of art as a whole then certainly of the art here in question. What one saw when one looked into the world as narrated by Aschenbach was elegant self-possession concealing inner dissolution and biological decay from the eyes of the world until the eleventh hour; a sallow, sensually destitute ugliness capable of fanning its smoldering lust into a pure flame, indeed, of rising to sovereignty in the realm of beauty; pallid impotence probing the incandescent depths of the mind for the strength to cast an entire supercilious people at the foot of the Cross, at *their* feet; an obliging manner in the empty, punctilious service of form; the life, false and dangerous, and the swiftly enervating desires and art of the born deceiver. Observing all this and much more of a like nature, one might well wonder whether the only possible heroism was the heroism of the weak. Yet what heroism was more at one with the times?

Gustav Aschenbach was the writer of all those who labor on the brink of exhaustion, the heavy-laden, the worn-down who yet hold their heads high, the moralists of achievement who, though slight of stature and chary of means, manage to attain, for a time at least, the trappings of greatness by combining rapture of the will with clever management. They are legion; they are the heroes of the age. And they all recognized themselves in his work, found themselves validated, celebrated, glorified therein; they rendered him thanks and proclaimed his name.

Young and green with the times and ill advised by them, he had stumbled in public, made false moves, made a fool of himself, violating tact and good sense in word and deed. Yet he eventually gained the dignity to which, as he maintained, every great talent feels instinctively drawn. One might even say that his entire development consisted in jettisoning the constraints of doubt and irony and making the conscious, defiant ascent to dignity.

Lively, intellectually undemanding formulations are the delight of the bourgeois masses, while passionately unbending youth is excited only by the problematic, and Aschenbach was as problematic and unbending as any youth. He had overindulged the intellect, overcultivated erudition and ground up the seed corn, revealed secrets, defamed talent, betrayed art; yes, even as his works entertained, elevated, and animated the gullible reader, he, the youthful artist, held the twenty-year-olds in thrall to his cynical remarks about the questionable nature of art and artistic genius.

Yet nothing would seem to dull a deft and noble intellect more swiftly, more surely than the sharp and bitter stimulant of erudition, and clearly the adolescent's melancholic and ever so conscientious thoroughness is shallow when compared with the profound resolve of the mature master to deny knowledge, disavow it, put it behind him, head high, lest it should in the slightest maim, discourage, or debase the will, action, feeling, and even passion. How is the celebrated "Wretched Figure" to be interpreted if not as an outburst of disgust with the indecent psychologizing of the age as embodied in the figure of a weak and fatuous semiscoundrel who fashions a destiny for himself by pushing his wife into the arms of a callow youth out of debility, depravity, or ethical laxity and then feels profoundly justified in committing base acts? The power of the word by which the outcast was cast out heralded a rejection of all moral doubt, all sympathy with the abyss, a renunciation of the leniency implicit in the homily claiming that to understand is to forgive, and what was under way here, indeed, what had come to pass was the "miraculous rebirth of impartiality," which surfaced a short time later with a certain mysterious urgency in one of the author's dialogues. Strange associations! Was it an intellectual consequence of this "rebirth," this new dignity and rigor, that at approximately this time critics observed an almost excessive intensification of his aesthetic sensibility, a noble purity, simplicity, and harmony of form that henceforth gave his artistic production so manifest, indeed, so calculated a stamp of virtuosity and classicism? But does not moral fortitude beyond knowledge— beyond disintegrative and inhibitory erudition—entail a simplification, a moral reduction of the world and the soul and hence a concomitant intensification of the will to evil, the forbidden, the morally reprehensible? And has not form a double face? Is it not moral and immoral at once—moral as the outcome and expression of discipline, yet immoral, even antimoral, insofar as it is by its very nature indifferent to morality, indeed, strives to bend morality beneath its proud and absolute scepter?

Be that as it may, development is destiny, and should it not take one course if lacking in the glamour and obligations of fame and another if attended by the interest and trust of a broad audience? Only incorrigible bohemians find it boring or laughable when a man of talent outgrows the libertine chrysalis stage and begins to perceive and express the dignity of the intellect, adopting the courtly ways of a solitude replete with bitter suffering and inner battles though eventually gaining a position of power and honor among men. And what sport, what bravado, what pleasure there is in fashioning one's own talent! As time progressed, Gustav Aschenbach's creations took on an official, didactic tone: in later years his style lost its brashness, its fresh, subtle nuances; it became fixed and exemplary, polished and conventional, conservative, formal, even formulaic, with the result that the aging man—like Louis XIV, if we are to believe tradition—banned all prosaic words from his vocabulary. It was then that school officials began including selected passages from his works in the textbooks they prescribed. He found it only fitting that a German prince who had just ascended the throne should confer nobility upon the author of *Frederick* on his fiftieth birthday, and he did not decline the honor.

After several restless years of testing this place and that, he eventually chose Munich as his permanent residence and led a solid bourgeois existence there, enjoying the respect that is in certain cases vouchsafed the intellect. The marriage he had contracted in his youth with a girl from a scholarly family was cut short, following a brief period of bliss, by the girl's death. It left him with a daughter, who was now married. He had had no son.

Gustav von Aschenbach was of somewhat less than medium height, dark, and clean-shaven. The head seemed a bit too large for the almost dainty physique. The hair, brushed back, was thin at the crown but very thick and gray at the temples and framed a high, rugged, scarred-looking forehead. The gold frame of the rimless spectacles cut into the root of a strong, nobly aquiline nose.

The mouth was large—now slack, now suddenly narrow and tight—the cheeks sunken and furrowed, the well-shaped chin slightly cleft. Important destinies must have passed through that head, which was often tilted dolefully, yet it was art—not, as is commonly the case, a hard and turbulent life—that had formed the physiognomy. The dazzling give and take of the interchange between Voltaire and the king on the subject of war had been conceived behind that brow; those eyes, wearily peering out through their lenses, had seen the gory inferno of the sick bays in the Seven Years War. On a personal level, too, art is life intensified: it delights more deeply, consumes more rapidly; it engraves the traces of imaginary and intellectual adventure on the countenance of its servant and in the long run, for all the monastic calm of his external existence, leads to self-indulgence, overrefinement, lethargy, and a restless curiosity that a lifetime of wild passions and pleasures could scarcely engender.

Three

Several matters of a mundane and literary nature kept him in Munich for approximately a fortnight after that walk, eager though he was to be on his way, but at last he gave orders for his country house to be made ready for occupancy within four weeks, and on a day between mid and late May he set off by night train for Trieste, where he tarried only twenty-four hours, boarding the ship for Pola the next morning.

What he sought was something exotic and distinctive yet of easy access, and so he stopped at an island in the Adriatic, not far from the coast of Istria, one that had acquired a following in recent years and featured colorful raggle-taggle rustics speaking an outlandish tongue and beautifully jagged cliffs facing the open sea. But rain, a heavy atmosphere, the provincial closed society of the Austrian hotel guests, and the lack of a peaceful, intimate rapport with the sea that only a soft, sandy beach can provide had soured him and kept him from feeling he had found his final destination. He was troubled by an impulse to go he knew not quite where, and he was studying the ships' timetables and looking hither and yon when all at once his goal, surprising yet at the same time self-evident, stared him in the face. Where did one go when one wished to travel overnight to a unique, fairy-tale-like location? Why, that was obvious. What was he doing here? He had come to the wrong place. That is where he should have gone. He lost no time in announcing his departure. A week and a half after his arrival on the island a swift motorboat bore him and his luggage across the misty morning water back to the naval base and he disembarked only to mount a gangplank leading to the damp deck of a steamer about to weigh anchor for Venice.

It was an ancient vessel of Italian registry, outdated, sooty, and drab. In a cavelike, artificially lit inner cabin, into which Aschenbach was ushered immediately after embarking by a decorously grinning, hunchbacked, grubby-looking old salt, he saw a man with a goatee and a hat pulled over his forehead, a cigarette butt hanging out of his mouth, and the face of an old-time circus director sitting at a desk recording the passengers' particulars and issuing them tickets with the slick, easygoing gestures of his trade. "Venice!" he said, repeating Aschenbach's request as he stretched out his arm and thrust his pen into the viscous dregs of a tilted inkwell. "Venice, first class! Certainly, sir!" And he scribbled something in large spindly letters, sprinkled blue sand from a box over it, let the sand run into a clay bowl, folded the paper with his bony yellow fingers, and wrote some more. "A fine choice!" he chattered all the while. "Ah, Venice! A magnificent city! A city irresistible to the man of culture for both its history and its current charms!" There was something numbing and distracting about the smooth rapidity of his movements and the empty prattle, as if he were worried the traveler would waver in his resolve to go to Venice. He quickly took Aschenbach's money and dropped the change on the stained tablecloth with the dexterity of a croupier. "Enjoy your stay, sir!" he said with a theatrical bow. "It has been an honor to serve you." Then he cried, "Next!" raising his arm immediately, as if business were brisk, though there was no one left needing attention. Aschenbach went back on deck.

With one arm propped on the railing he watched first the idlers loitering on the quay to watch the ship set sail, then the passengers on board. The second-class passengers, men and women both, were squatting on the forward deck, using their crates and bundles as rests. A group of young men on the upper deck, Pola shop assistants by the look of them, excited by the prospect of a jaunt to Italy, were making a great to-do about themselves and their venture, jabbering, laughing, indulging smugly in their gesticulations, and leaning over the railing to shout glib jeers at their friends, who were moving along the embankment, clutching their briefcases and shaking their canes menacingly at the holidaymakers. One of them, wearing an extravagantly cut pale-yellow summer suit, a red necktie, and a rakishly uptilted Panama hat, outdid the others in his raucous show of mirth. Once Aschenbach had had a closer look at him, however, he realized with something akin to horror that the man was no youth. He was old, there was no doubting it: he had wrinkles around his eyes and mouth; the matt crimson of his cheeks was rouge; the brown hair beneath the straw hat with its colorful band— a toupee; the neck—scrawny, emaciated; the stuck-on mustache and imperial on his chin—dyed; the full complement of yellow teeth—a cheap denture; and the hands, with signet rings on both forefingers, those of an old man. A shudder ran through Aschenbach as he watched him and his interplay with his friends. Did they not know, could they not see that he was old, that he had no right to be wearing their foppish, gaudy clothes, no right to be carrying on as if he were one of them? They seemed to be used to him and take him for granted, tolerating his presence and treating him as an equal, returning his pokes in the ribs without malice. How could they? Aschenbach laid his hand on his forehead and shut his eyes: they felt hot for want of sleep. He had the impression that something was not quite normal, that a dreamlike disaffection, a warping of the world into something alien was about to take hold and that by covering his face for a spell and then taking a fresh look at things he might stave it off. Just then, however, he felt a floating sensation and, looking up panic-stricken, realized that the heavy, dingy bulk of the ship was slowly casting off from the stone jetty. As the engine shifted forward and back, the strip of filthy, shimmering water between the jetty and the ship's hull increased inch by inch, and after some clumsy maneuvering the steamer aimed its bowsprit at the open sea. Aschenbach crossed to the starboard side, where the hunchback had set up a deck chair for him and a steward in a stained frock coat inquired whether he could do anything for him.

The sky was gray, the wind humid. Harbor and islands left behind, all land soon disappeared from sight in the haze. Flakes of coal dust, bloated with moisture, settled on the swabbed deck, which refused to dry. Before an hour was up, a sailcloth awning was spread out: it had started to rain.

Wrapped in his coat, a book in his lap, the traveler took his ease, the hours slipping by unnoticed. The rain had ceased; the awning been taken down. The horizon was now visible in its entirety. The vast disk of the barren sea stretched out beneath the turbid dome of the sky. But in empty, unarticulated space our senses lose the capacity to articulate time as well, and we sink into the immeasurable. Strange, shadowy figures—the superannuated dandy, the goateed purser from deep in the hold—passed through his quiescent mind with vague gestures and jumbled dreamlike utterances, and he fell asleep.

At noon he was urged to partake of a collation below in the dining salon, which was nothing so much as a corridor lined with cabin doors and where at the other end of the long table—he sat at its head—the shop assistants, the old man included, had been tippling with the jovial captain since ten o'clock. The meal was wretched, and he finished it off quickly: he felt the need for fresh air, for a look at the sky. Surely it would clear over Venice.

Not that he thought it would not, for the city had always received him in all its glory. Yet both sky and sea remained turbid and leaden, a misty rain falling from time to time, and he resigned himself to finding a different Venice by sea from the one he was accustomed to find when taking an overland route. He stood at the foremast, gazing into the distance, watching for land. He thought of the pensive yet ardent poet for whom the cupolas and bell towers of his dreams had once risen from these waves, repeated to himself the words he had fashioned out of reverence, joy, and mourning into measured song, and, readily stirred by a sentiment already shaped, probed his earnest, weary heart to see whether a new ardor and upheaval, a belated adventure of the emotions might yet await the idle traveler.

Then, to the right, the flat coastline hove in sight, the sea came alive with fishing boats, and the island with its swimming baths appeared. The steamer put the island on its port side and glided at reduced speed through the narrow channel that bore its name, coming to a halt in the lagoon opposite some colorfully dilapidated dwellings, there to await the launch of the health authorities.

It took the launch an hour to appear. The ship had arrived, yet it had not. There was no hurry, yet the passengers were impatient. The young men from Pola, their patriotism stimulated by the military bugle calls crossing the water from the vicinity of the Public Gardens, had come on deck and, full of Asti-induced ebullience, were cheering on the *bersaglieri* drilling there. But it was repugnant to behold the state to which the spruced-up fossil had been reduced by his spurious coalition with the young. His brain was too old to withstand the wine as his youthfully resilient companions had done: he was miserably drunk. Eyes glazed over, a cigarette between his trembling fingers, he swayed back and forth in his inebriation, laboriously keeping his balance. Since he would have fallen at the first step, he did not dare move, yet he displayed a pitiful exuberance, buttonholing everyone who came up to him, jabbering, winking, sniggering, lifting a wrinkled, ringed finger as a part of some fatuous teasing, and licking the corners of his mouth with the tip of his tongue in a revoltingly suggestive manner. Aschenbach watched him with a frown, and once more a feeling of numbness came over him, as if the world were moving ever so slightly yet intractably towards a strange and grotesque warping, a feeling which circumstances kept him from indulging in, however, because at that moment the pounding of the engine started up again and the ship, interrupted so near its destination, resumed its course through the San Marco Canal.

And so he saw it once again, that most astounding of landing sites, that stunning composition of fantastic architecture offered up by the Republic to the reverent gaze of approaching seafarers, the ethereal splendor of the Palace and the Bridge of Sighs, the waterside columns with lion and saint, the majestically projecting flank of the fairy-tale basilica, and the view beyond of the gateway and giant clock, and taking it all in he mused that arriving in Venice by land, at the railway station, was tantamount to entering a palace by the back door and that one should approach this most improbable of cities only as he had now done by ship, over the seas.

The engine stopped, gondolas pressed alongside, the gangplank was lowered, and customs officials came aboard and discharged their duties perfunctorily: disembarkation could proceed. Aschenbach let it be known that he wished to have a gondola convey him and his luggage to the pier of those vaporetti that ply between the city and the Lido, for he intended to take up residence by the sea. His plan was approved, his request shouted to the water below, where the gondoliers were squabbling in dialect. He was held back from leaving, held back by his trunk, which had to be laboriously dragged to and tugged down the ladderlike steps. He was thus unable to elude the importunities of the ghastly old man, who felt impelled by some obscure drunken urge to officiate over the stranger's departure. "We wish you a most pleasant stay," he bleated, bowing and scraping. "We hope you remember us. *Au revoir, excusez,* and *bonjour,* Your Excellency!" He drooled, he squinted, he licked the corners of his mouth, and the dyed imperial on his old man's chin jutted into the air. "Our compliments," he babbled on, placing two fingers to his lips, "to your sweetheart, your sweet, your most beautiful sweetheart . . ." And suddenly the upper denture slipped out of his jaw over the lower lip. Aschenbach managed to escape. "Your sweetheart, your lovely sweetheart," came the cooing, hollow, garbled words behind him as he made his way down the gangplank, clutching the rope railing.

Who has not battled a fleeting shudder, a secret dread and anxiety upon boarding a Venetian gondola for the first time or after a prolonged absence? That strange conveyance, coming down to us unaltered from the days of the ballads and so distinctively black, black as only coffins can be—it conjures up hush-hush criminal adventures in the rippling night and, even more, death itself: the bier, the obscure obsequies, the final, silent journey. And has anyone observed that the seat in such a boat, that armchair lacquered coffin-black with its dull black upholstery, is the softest, most soothing, most voluptuous seat in the world? Aschenbach grew aware of this after settling down at the gondolier's feet opposite his luggage, which lay neatly assembled in the prow. The rowers were still squabbling, raucous and unintelligible, gesturing menacingly, but the strange silence of this city of water seemed to absorb their voices gently, disembody them, and scatter them over the sea. It was warm here in the harbor. Lulled by the tepid breath of the sirocco, lolling on the cushions over the pliant element, the traveler closed his eyes and yielded to a lassitude as unwonted as it was sweet. "The ride will be brief," he thought. "Could it but last forever." Rocking tranquilly, he felt himself drift away from the throng and the jumble of voices.

How calm and yet calmer his surroundings became! There was nothing to be heard but the plash of the oar and the hollow thump of the waves against the prow, which rose up over the water, steep and black and reinforced at the tip like a halberd, and yet a third sound, a mutter, a murmur, the whisper of the gondolier talking to himself through clenched teeth, in fits and starts, the sounds extracted by the effort of his arms. Aschenbach glanced up and noted not without consternation that the lagoon was widening about him and the gondola making for the open sea. Clearly he could not relax all that much; he would have to see to the execution of his wishes.

"To the vaporetto pier, I told you!" he said, half turning. The murmuring ceased, but no reply was forthcoming.

"To the vaporetto pier, I said!" he repeated, turning all the way round and peering up into the face of the gondolier, who loomed behind him on his raised plank against the pallid sky. He had a disobliging, even brutal physiognomy and was dressed in navy blue, with a yellow sash wound round his waist and a shapeless straw hat that was beginning to unravel perched jauntily on his head. The cast of the face and the curly blond mustache under the small snub nose made him look anything but Italian. Though rather frailly built—one would not have thought him particularly suited to his trade—he handled the oar with great energy, putting his whole body into every stroke. From time to time, his lips drawn back by the strain, he bared a set of white teeth. Knitting his reddish eyebrows, he looked over his charge's head and retorted in curt, almost churlish tones, "You are going to the Lido."

"I am," Aschenbach parried, "but I hired the gondola to take me only as far as San Marco. I wish to transfer to the vaporetto."

"You cannot transfer to the vaporetto, sir."

"And why not?"

"Because the vaporetto takes no luggage."

That was so, Aschenbach remembered. He said nothing, but the gruff, preemptory manner, so unlike the treatment foreigners usually receive from the natives, he found disagreeable.

"That is my business," he said. "Perhaps I wish to deposit my luggage there. You will turn back."

Silence. The oar plashed; the water thudded against the prow. Presently the muttering and murmuring commenced again: the gondolier was talking to himself between his teeth.

What was he to do? Alone on the water with this oddly obstreperous, uncannily determined man, the traveler saw no way of imposing his will. Besides, what a nice rest he could have if he did not lose his temper! Had he not wished the trip to last longer, last forever? It was wisest to let things take their course; what is more, it was highly pleasant. A spellbinding indolence seemed to emanate from his seat, that low armchair upholstered in black, so gently rocked by the oar strokes of the self-willed gondolier behind him. The idea that he had fallen into the hands of a criminal drifted dreamily through Aschenbach's mind, but it was powerless to stir him to active resistance. More upsetting was the possibility that it could all be put down to simple money grubbing. A sense of duty or pride, the recollection, as it were, that one might forestall such things, moved him to pull himself together, and he asked, "What do you charge for the trip?"

Looking straight past him, the gondolier answered, "You will pay."

The response called for was clear. "I shall not pay a thing," Aschenbach answered mechanically, "not a thing if you take me where I do not want to go."

"You want to go to the Lido."

"But not with you."

"I am rowing you well."

Fair enough, thought Aschenbach, relaxing. Fair enough. You are rowing me well. Even if you are after my purse and send me to the House of Hades with a bash of the oar from behind, you will have rowed me well.

But nothing of the sort occurred. They even had company: a boatload of musical highwaymen, men and women both, singing to a guitar and a mandolin and sailing solicitously alongside the gondola, filling the stillness over the waters with their venal for-foreigners-only poetry. Aschenbach tossed some money into the hat they held out. They immediately fell silent and departed, whereupon he could hear the gondolier whispering again, carrying on his intermittent conversation with himself.

And so they arrived, bobbing in the wake of a vaporetto bound for the city. Two municipal officials, their hands behind their backs, were pacing up and down the embankment, looking out over the lagoon. Aschenbach left the gondola at the landing stage, assisted by the old man with a grappling iron to be found at every landing stage in Venice, and, having run out of coins, crossed to the hotel opposite the pier to break a banknote and give the oarsman his just deserts. After being attended to in the lobby, he returned to find his belongings on a cart on the pier and the gondola and gondolier gone, nowhere to be seen.

"He took off," said the old man with the grappling iron. "A bad lot that man. He had no license, sir. The only gondolier without one. The others phoned over to us. He saw the officials waiting for him, so he took off."

Aschenbach shrugged.

"You got a free ride, sir," the old man said, holding

his hat out. Aschenbach tossed some coins into it. He gave instructions for his luggage to be taken to the Hôtel des Bains and followed the cart along the avenue, the white-blossoming tree-lined avenue which, flanked by taverns, bazaars, and boardinghouses, ran straight across the island to the beach.

He entered the spacious hotel from the back, the garden terrace, and made his way through the spacious lobby and vestibule to the office. Since he was expected, he was received with assiduous deference. The manager, a short, quiet, obsequiously courteous man sporting a black mustache and a frock coat of French cut, rode up to the second floor with him and showed him to his room, a pleasant place furnished with cherry-wood furniture and decorated with strongly scented flowers, its high windows offering a view of the open sea. He walked up to one of them after the manager had withdrawn, and while his luggage was being brought in and set down behind him he gazed out at the beach, which was all but devoid of people, it being afternoon, and the sunless sea, which at high tide was sending long, low waves against the shore in a calm, regular cadence.

The observations and encounters of a man of solitude and few words are at once more nebulous and
more intense than those of a gregarious man, his
thoughts more ponderable, more bizarre and never
without a hint of sadness. Images and perceptions that
might easily be dismissed with a glance, a laugh, an
exchange of opinions occupy him unduly; they are
heightened in the silence, gain in significance, turn into
experience, adventure, emotion. Solitude begets origi-
nality, bold and disconcerting beauty, poetry. But solitude can also beget perversity, disparity, the absurd and
the forbidden. Accordingly, the figures encountered on
the journey—the repulsive old fop with his "sweetheart" drivel, the outlaw gondolier defrauded of his
fee—still rankled in the traveler's mind. Though neither difficult to explain rationally nor even thought-
provoking, they were utterly outlandish—or so he
found them—and unsettling precisely because of this
paradox. For the moment, however, he greeted the sea
with his eyes, delighted that Venice was so near and
easy of access, and at length he turned, washed his face,
gave the chambermaid instructions for seeing to his

comfort, and had himself conveyed by the green-clad Swiss lift attendant to the ground floor.

He took his tea on the seaside terrace, then went down and walked a good distance along the promenade in the direction of the Hotel Excelsior. Upon his return he thought it time to change for dinner. He did so in his usual slow and deliberate manner, for he was accustomed to work while attending to his toilet, yet he reached the lobby a bit too early, finding a goodly number of the guests, strangers to one another, feigning mutual indifference as they waited together for the meal. He picked up a newspaper from the table, settled into a leather armchair, and cast an eye over the company, which differed favorably from that of his previous hotel.

A broad, tolerant, all-encompassing horizon opened before him. Sounds of the major languages mingled in muted tones. Internationally recognized evening dress, that uniform of civilization, made of the diversity a semblance of homogeneous decency. He saw the dry, long face of an American, a large Russian clan, English ladies, and German children with French nurses. The

Slav element seemed to prevail. Polish was being spoken in his immediate vicinity.

It came from a group of young people of various ages seated around a wicker table under the supervision of a governess or female companion: three girls, between the ages of fifteen and seventeen from the looks of them, and a long-haired boy of about fourteen. Aschenbach noted with astonishment that the boy was of a consummate beauty: his face—pale and charmingly reticent, ringed by honey-colored hair, with a straight nose, lovely mouth, and an expression of gravity sweet and divine—recalled Greek statuary of the noblest period, yet its purest formal perfection notwithstanding it conveyed a unique personal charm such that whoever might gaze upon it would believe he had never beheld anything so accomplished, be it in nature or in art. Also striking were the clear and fundamental differences in the approach to child rearing that appeared to govern the dress and general behavior of the siblings. The attire of the three girls, the eldest of whom could be considered grown up, was austere and chaste to the point of defacement: their identical habitlike, slate-colored, knee-length dresses, sober and deliberately unbecoming in cut and brightened only by white turndown collars, suppressed and nullified any grace they might have had. Their hair, plastered down smoothly over their heads, made their faces as vacant and inexpressive as a nun's. Surely a mother was at work here, and one who had no intention of applying to the boy the strict pedagogical principles she deemed appropriate to the girls. In his life, softness and tenderness clearly held sway. His fair hair had been spared the shears: as in *Boy with Thorn* it curled down over his forehead and ears and still lower onto his neck. The English sailor's suit—with its puffy sleeves narrowing to tight circles around the dainty wrists of the still childlike but slender hands and its braiding, bows, and embroideries—gave his delicate figure a rich and pampered appearance. He sat half facing his observer with one black patent leather shoe in front of the other, an elbow propped on the arm of his wicker chair, and a cheek resting against the closed hand in an attitude of nonchalant propriety and completely devoid of the all but servile rigidity to which his female siblings seemed accustomed. Was he ailing? His complexion stood out white as ivory against the darker gold of the surrounding curls. Or was he merely the coddled favorite, the object of a biased and volatile love? Aschenbach inclined towards the latter. Innate in nearly every artistic nature is a wanton, treacherous penchant for accepting injustice when it creates beauty and showing sympathy for and paying homage to aristocratic privilege.

A waiter made the rounds, announcing in English that dinner was served, and the guests gradually disappeared through the glass door. Latecomers straggled past from the vestibule and lifts. Service had begun in the dining room, but the young Poles lingered at their wicker table, and Aschenbach, comfortably ensconced in his deep armchair and admiring the beauty before his eyes besides, waited with them.

The governess—a short, corpulent, red-faced woman of not quite gentle birth—signaled them at last to rise. Arching her brows, she pushed her chair back and bowed when a tall woman dressed in grayish white and richly adorned with pearls entered the lobby. The woman's demeanor was cool and dignified; the look of her lightly powdered coiffure and the cut of her dress displayed the simplicity that prescribes taste wherever piety is deemed an attribute of aristocracy. She could have been the wife of a high-ranking German official. The only aspect of her appearance evincing a certain fanciful sense of luxury was the jewelry, which was in fact nearly worthless and consisted of earrings plus a very long triple strand of gently shimmering pearls the size of cherries.

The siblings had risen quickly. They bent to kiss the hand of their mother, who, a reserved smile on her well-preserved yet somewhat weary and pointy-nosed face, looked past their heads and addressed a few words in French to the governess. Then she went over to the glass door. The children followed, the girls in order of age, the governess, and finally the boy. For some reason he looked back before crossing the threshold, and since there was no one else left in the lobby, his eyes, of an unusual twilight gray, met those of Aschenbach, who, his paper in his lap, was absorbed in watching the group make its exit.

There was certainly nothing the least bit remarkable about what he had seen. The children had not gone in before their mother; they had waited for her, greeted her deferentially, and observed the customary formalities when entering the dining room. Yet it had all been done so deliberately, with such concern for discipline, duty, and self-esteem that Aschenbach felt strangely moved. He hesitated a few moments more, then he too made his way to the dining room and was shown to his table, which, he noted with a brief stir of regret, was at some remove from that of the Polish family.

Tired yet mentally alert, he whiled away the lengthy meal pondering abstract, even transcendental matters such as the mysterious connection that must be established between the generic and the particular to produce human beauty and moving on to general problems of form and art only to conclude that his thoughts and discoveries resembled certain seemingly felicitous revelations that come to us in dreams and after sober consideration prove perfectly inane and worthless. He lingered after dinner—sitting and smoking, strolling through the hotel grounds enjoying the evening fragrance—then retired early and spent the night in a deep sleep, unbroken, yet animated by a number of dreams.

The weather had not improved the next morning. The wind came from the land. The sea was dull and calm, shrunken almost, under a pale, overcast sky, the horizon blandly close; the sea had retreated so far from the beach that it left several rows of long sandbanks exposed. Opening his window, Aschenbach thought he could smell the foul stench of the lagoon.

A sudden despondency came over him. He considered leaving then and there. Once, years before, after weeks of a beautiful spring, he had been visited by this sort of weather and it so affected his health he had been obliged to flee. Was not the same listless fever setting in? The pressure in the temples, the heavy eyelids? Changing hotels again would be a nuisance, but if the wind failed to shift he could not possibly remain here. To be on the safe side, he did not unpack everything. At nine he went to breakfast in the specially designated buffet between the lobby and the dining room.

The ceremonious silence on which grand hotels pride themselves prevailed. The waiters moved about the room noiselessly, on tiptoe. The clatter of tea things and a half-whispered word were the only sounds audible. In a corner diagonally opposite the door and two tables removed from his own, Aschenbach saw the Polish girls with their governess. Their ash-blond hair freshly plastered down, their eyes red, they sat perfectly erect in their stiff blue-linen dress with the small white turndown collars and cuffs, passing a jar of preserves round the table. The boy was absent.

Aschenbach smiled. Well, well, little Phaeacian! he thought. You seem to be the only one privileged to sleep his fill. And brightening suddenly, he recited the following line to himself: "Oft did they change their garments and bathe in warm water, reclining."

He took a leisurely breakfast, was given some forwarded mail by the porter—who had entered the room, braided cap in hand—then smoked a cigarette and opened one or two of the letters. And so it transpired that he was present for the entrance of the slug-abed awaited in the corner.

He came through the glass door and walked straight across the quiet room to his sisters' table. His gait was extraordinarily graceful both in the way he held his upper torso and in the way he moved his knees and white-shod feet; it was a very light gait, at once delicate and proud, and embellished by the childlike modesty with which, twice on his way across the room, he turned his head and raised, then lowered his eyes. Smiling and murmuring a word in his soft, fuzzy language, he took his seat, and now, especially as he had turned his full profile to the observer, the latter was once more amazed, indeed, startled by the truly godlike beauty of this mortal being. Today the boy was wearing a lightweight, washable outfit with a blue-and-white-striped middy blouse that had a red silk bow at the chest and a plain white stand-up collar. The collar, though none too elegant a match for the rest of the outfit, showed off the boy's fair, blossoming head in its consummate charm, the head of an Eros with the creamy glaze of Parian marble, eyebrows serious and finely traced, temples and ear covered darkly and softly at right angles by encroaching ringlets.

Good, good, thought Aschenbach with that cool, professional approval in which artists encountering a masterpiece sometimes shroud their delight, their excitement. Truth to tell, he went on thinking, were sea and shore not awaiting me, I should stay here as long as you! But he did leave, greeted by the staff as he passed through the lobby, then descending the large terrace and proceeding straight along the boardwalk to the beach partitioned off for the hotel guests. He was shown to his rented cabana by the barefoot old man in linen trousers, sailor's tunic, and straw hat serving there as bathing attendant, had his table and chair set up on a sandy wooden platform, and made himself comfortable in the chaise longue he had drawn onto the wax-yellow sand closer to the water.

The view of the beach, the spectacle of civilization indulging in carefree sensuality on the brink of the watery element, entertained and pleased him as rarely before. The flat gray sea was already alive with wading children, swimmers, and colorful figures lying on sandbars, their arms crossed under their heads. Others were rowing small keelless boats painted red and blue, laughing as they capsized. The long row of cabanas, which had platforms like miniature verandahs for people to sit on, was a scene of animated activity and idly protracted repose, visits and chatter, meticulous matitudinal elegance

alongside a nakedness unabashedly enjoying the free-
doms of the place. Further out on the moist, firm sand
there were individuals strolling in white bathing robes
or loose, brightly colored frocks. On the right, an intri-
cate sand castle built by children was bedecked with
small flags in the colors of all nations; vendors hawked
mussels, pastries, and fruit, kneeling before their wares.
On the left, in front of one of the cabanas set at right
angles to the others and to the sea and thus closing off
that side of the beach, a Russian family had set up
camp—men with beards and big teeth; listless, submis-
sive women; a Baltic spinster seated at an easel and
emitting cries of despair as she painted the sea; two ugly,
good-natured children; and an old nanny in a kerchief, with the gentle, servile manner of a slave. They
were cheerful and having great fun, tirelessly shouting
the names of the romping, unruly children, using the
few Italian words at their disposal to joke with the
amusing old man from whom they bought sweets,
kissing one another on the cheeks, and caring never a
whit whether their very human esprit de corps was
being observed.

"I shall stay, then," Aschenbach thought. "What better place could there be?" And folding his hands in his lap, he let his eyes run over the sea's great expanse and set his gaze adrift till it blurred and broke in the monotonous mist of barren space. He loved the sea and for deep-seated reasons: the hardworking artist's need for repose, the desire to take shelter from the demanding diversity of phenomena in the bosom of boundless simplicity, a propensity—proscribed and diametrically opposed to his mission in life and for that very reason seductive—a propensity for the unarticulated, the immoderate, the eternal, for nothingness. To repose in perfection is the desire of all those who strive for excellence, and is not nothingness a form of perfection? But as he dreamt his way deep into the void, the horizontal shoreline was suddenly intersected by a human form and, summoning his gaze back from the infinite and bringing it into focus, he saw none other than the beautiful boy coming from the left, walking past him in the sand. He was barefoot in preparation for wading, his slender legs exposed to above the knee, and while his gait was slow it was as light and proud as if he were quite accustomed to going about shoeless. He looked over at the cabanas in the perpendicular row, but no sooner did he spy the Russian family going about its business in cheerful harmony than a storm cloud of angry disdain came over his face: the forehead wrinkled into a dark frown; the mouth rose up, pulling the lips to one side in a bitter grimace that rent the cheek; the brows grew so deeply furrowed that the eyes seemed to have sunk under the pressure, glowering out from beneath them, speaking the language of hate. He looked down, looked back again ominously, then thrust one shoulder forward in a show of repulsion and rebuff, and left his enemies behind.

A kind of delicacy or apprehension, something akin to deference or modesty, caused Aschenbach to turn away, as if he had seen nothing. Any serious individual who chances to observe a moment of passion is loath to make personal use of what he has witnessed. Yet he was cheered and shaken at the same time, in other words, elated. This childish fanaticism aimed at so benign a target gave the boy's mute divinity a human perspective: it made an exquisite work of nature—a statue, a mere feast for the eyes—something worthy of deeper consideration and placed the figure of an adolescent, already remarkable for his beauty, against a background enabling one to take him seriously beyond his years.

His eyes still averted, Aschenbach listened to the boy's voice, the high, rather weak voice with which, still some way off, he greeted his playmates, who were busy building a sand castle. They responded, calling out his name or pet name several times, and Aschenbach listened to it with a certain curiosity, but could make out nothing more than two melodic syllables: "Adgio" or, more often, "Adgiu," with a final *u* they lengthened as they called. He liked the sound of it: he found its euphony appropriate to the object in question and, having repeated it to himself, turned back, contented, to his letters and papers.

With his portable writing case on his knees, he began attending to this or that item of correspondence with his fountain pen. But after no more than a quarter of an hour he decided it was a pity to divert his mind from the situation at hand, the most enjoyable he knew, to let it slip past for the sake of an indifferent pursuit. He tossed his writing utensils aside and gazed back at the sea, but before long, distracted by the voices of the youngsters building the sand castle, he placidly turned his head to the right along the back of the chair the better to follow once more the doings of the exquisite Adgio.

He located him at once: the red bow on his chest was unmistakable. Engaged with the others in laying an old plank as a bridge across the sand castle's water-filled moat, he gave directions by shouts and head signals. He had ten or so companions, boys and girls—some his own age, some younger—chattering higgledy-piggledy in tongues: Polish, French, and even some Balkan languages. But his name was the most often heard. He was clearly sought after, courted, admired. One boy in particular, a Pole like him—a stocky fellow who was addressed as something like Jasiu and who had black, slicked-down hair and was wearing a belted linen suit—appeared to be his closest vassal and friend. When the current stage of work on the castle came to an end, they walked along the beach with their arms around each other, and the fellow addressed as Jasiu kissed the beautiful youth.

Aschenbach was tempted to shake a finger at them. "I advise you, Critobulus," he thought with a smile, "to travel for a year. For you will need at least that long to recover." Then he breakfasted on some large, fully ripe strawberries he had purchased from a peddler. It had grown very hot, though the sun was unable to pierce the layer of haze in the sky. Lethargy fettered the mind even as the senses enjoyed the vast, benumbing pleasure of the ocean's calm. The serious Aschenbach found it a suitable, perfectly satisfying use of his time to guess at or postulate on the name that sounded like Adgio, and with the aid of some Polish reminiscences he determined that it must be Tadzio, the pet name for Tadeusz, which becomes Tadziu in direct address.*

Tadzio was bathing. Aschenbach, who had lost sight of him, spotted his head, then his arm rising paddlelike from the water far out at sea, the sea being most likely shallow for quite a distance. But already he seemed a cause for concern; already women's voices were calling out to him from the cabanas, once more shouting the

* Likewise, Jasiu is the direct-address form of the name of Tadzio's friend Jaś, which is the pet name for Jan. (Translator's note)

name that dominated the beach almost like a catchword, its soft consonants and long-drawn-out final *u* making it at once sweet and wild: "Tadziu! Tadziu!" Back he came, running through the waves, his legs beating the resistant water into foam, his head flung back, and to see so vibrant a figure, with the grace and austerity of early manhood, locks dripping, fair as a gentle god, emerging from the depths of sea and sky, escaping the watery element—it was enough to inspire mythical associations, like the lay of a bard about times primeval, about the origin of form and the birth of the gods. His eyes closed, Aschenbach harkened to the chant welling up within him and thought again that being here was good and he would stay.

Later Tadzio lay in the sand resting from his swim, wrapped in a white sheet drawn up under his right shoulder, his head reposing on a bare arm, and Aschenbach—even when not observing him, when reading a few pages in his book—hardly ever forgot that he was there and that he had only to turn his head slightly to the right to glimpse the object of his admiration. He almost felt he was sitting there to keep watch over the boy as he rested—indulging in his own affairs, yet constantly guarding the noble figure a little way off to his right. And he was infused with a paternal affection, the attraction that one who begets beauty by means of self-sacrifice feels for one who is inherently beautiful.

After midday he left the beach, returned to the hotel, and went up to his room. There he spent quite some time before the mirror, studying his gray hair and pinched, weary face. Reflecting the while on his fame— people often recognized him on the street and gazed after him respectfully for the unerring precision and grace of his diction—he evoked all the outward signs of success he owed to his talent, even his noble title. He then went down to the dining room for lunch at his table. When he entered the lift after the meal, a group of young people also coming from lunch crowded into the floating cubicle after him, Tadzio amongst them. He stood quite close to Aschenbach, so close that for the first time he perceived him not as a distant work of art and, given the minute detail, acknowledged his human qualities. Someone addressed the boy, and while replying, with an indescribably winsome smile, he backed out

at the next floor, his eyes cast down. Beauty breeds dif-
fidence, thought Aschenbach, earnestly wondering why.
He had noticed, however, that Tadzio's teeth were less
than attractive: a bit jagged and pale, lacking the gleam
of health, and with that brittle, transparent quality sometimes found in anemics. He is very frail, he is sickly,
thought Aschenbach. He'll probably not live long. And
he made no attempt to account for why he felt satisfied
or consoled at the thought.

He spent two hours in his room and took the vaporetto across the foul-smelling lagoon to Venice in the
afternoon. He got out at San Marco, had tea in the
square, and then, in conformity with his daily program
there, set off on a stroll through the streets. But this
stroll brought about a major change in his mood and
intentions.

A repellent sultriness permeated the narrow
streets, the air so thick that the odors emanating from
houses, shops, and food stalls—the vapor of oil, the
clouds of perfume, and more—hovered like fumes
without dispersing. Cigarette smoke hung in place,
dissipating slowly. Aschenbach felt more irritated than

invigorated by the bustle of the crowd. The longer he walked, the more afflicted he was by that odious condition brought on by the combination of sea air and sirocco: simultaneous excitation and prostration. He broke out into a disagreeable sweat. His eyes refused to function, his chest constricted, he felt feverish, the blood throbbed in his head. He fled the bustling commercial streets and crossed the bridges into the alleyways of the poor. There he was set upon by beggars, and the fetid effluvia from the canals made breathing a torment. Leaning against the edge of a fountain in a quiet square, one of those forgotten, godforsaken spots in the heart of Venice, he wiped his forehead and realized he would have to travel on.

For the second time—and this time definitively—the city had proved itself extremely harmful to him in such weather. Braving it out obstinately seemed unreasonable, the prospect of a shift in the wind being quite uncertain. An immediate decision was of the essence. Returning home was out of the question at this point: neither his summer nor his winter quarters were ready. But this was not the only place with sea and sand, and elsewhere they were to be had without the nefarious admixture of the lagoon and its feverous vapors. He recalled having heard the praises of a small seaside resort not far from Trieste. Why not go there? And without delay, to make the move to yet another locale worth the effort. He rose, resolute, to his feet. At the next gondola stop he boarded a boat and was rowed through the murky labyrinth of the canals under graceful marble balconies flanked by carved lions, around corners of slimy masonry, past funereal palazzo façades, their large commercial signs mirrored in the bobbing water strewn with refuse, and on to San Marco. He had some difficulty getting there, because the gondolier, in league as he was with the lace factories and glass works, kept trying to stop so he might view and purchase their wares, and whenever the bizarre journey through Venice began to cast its spell upon him the cutpurse mercantilism of the sunken queen did its part to bring him painfully back to his senses.

Upon his return to the hotel, even before dining, he informed the office that unforeseen circumstances had compelled him to leave early the following morning.

Regrets were tendered, the bill settled. He dined and spent the warm evening reading newspapers in a rocking chair on the back terrace. Before retiring, he packed all his belongings for departure.

He did not sleep particularly well, the imminent displacement having unnerved him. When he opened the windows in the morning, the sky was as overcast as it had been, but the air seemed fresher, and—regret set in. Had giving notice not been impetuous and wrongheaded, the result of an inconsequential indisposition? If he had held off a bit, if he had not been so quick to lose heart, if he had instead tried to adjust to the air or wait for the weather to improve, he would now have been free of stress and strain and looking forward to a morning on the beach like the one the day before. Too late. He must go on wanting what he had wanted yesterday. He dressed and rode down to the ground floor at eight for breakfast.

The breakfast room was still empty when he went in. Several guests arrived while he sat waiting for his order. His teacup at his lips, he watched the Polish girls enter with their companion. Stiff and fresh from sleep, their eyes still red, they proceeded to their table in the corner near the window. Shortly thereafter the porter went up to him, cap in hand, to admonish him to depart: the motorcar was ready to drive the gentleman and several other passengers to the Hotel Excelsior, where the motor launch would be waiting to convey them to the station via the company's private canal. Time was pressing.

Aschenbach felt time was doing nothing of the sort: his train was not due to leave for more than an hour. He resented the way hotels prevailed upon their guests to vacate the premises prematurely and indicated to the porter that he wished to breakfast in peace. The man withdrew hesitantly only to reappear five minutes later. The motorcar could not possibly wait any longer, he said. Then let it go and take his trunk with it, Aschenbach retorted angrily; he would use the public vaporetto when the time came, and would he kindly leave the arrangements for his departure to him? The employee bowed. Glad to have fended off the man's tedious admonitions, Aschenbach finished his breakfast in a leisurely fashion; he even had the waiter bring him a newspaper. Time was indeed short by the time he stood at last. And it so happened that at that very instant Tadzio entered through the glass door.

As he crossed the departing Aschenbach's path on his way to the family table, he modestly lowered his eyes before the man with the gray hair and lofty brow only to raise them again, soft and wide, in that charming way of his, and walk past. "Adieu, Tadzio!" Aschenbach thought. "It was all too brief." And, contrary to his custom, actually forming the words with his lips and uttering them to himself, he added, "God bless you."

He then went through the departure formalities—distributing gratuities and listening to the short, soft-spoken manager in the French frock coat make his farewell—left the hotel on foot as he had come, followed by the hotel porter with his hand luggage, and set out for the vaporetto landing along the white-blossoming avenue that cut across the island. Having reached it, he took a seat—and what ensued was a woeful calvary through the depths of remorse.

It was the familiar ride across the lagoon, past San Marco and up the Grand Canal. Aschenbach sat on the curved bench in the bow, an arm on the railing and a hand shading his eyes. The Public Gardens faded into the distance, and the Piazzetta once more displayed its princely elegance, but it, too, retreated, and after a great rush of palazzi the splendid marble arch of the Rialto came into view around a bend in the waterway. The traveler looked on, his breast riven. The atmosphere of the city, that faintly fetid odor of sea and swamp he had been so anxious to flee—he now breathed it in, in deep, delicately throbbing drafts. Was it possible he had not known or even considered how much it all meant to him? What that morning had been a pang of sorrow, a vague doubt as to the validity of his actions was now grief, true pain, an affliction of the soul so bitter that it brought tears to his eyes more than once and, as he told himself, was totally unforeseen. What he found so hard to bear and even utterly intolerable at times was clearly the thought that he would never see Venice again, that this was a farewell forever. For now that the city had twice made him ill, now that he had twice been forced to pick up and leave it, he would henceforth be obliged to consider it an impossible and forbidden destination, one he was not up to and could never think of revisiting. Indeed, he felt that should he leave now, shame and pride must prevent him from setting eyes again on the beloved city that had twice brought him low, and this conflict between the soul's inclination and the body's capabilities suddenly struck the aging man as so serious and significant, his physical defeat seemed so ignominious, in such urgent need of redress, that he could not comprehend the frivolous resignation with which he had decided to acknowledge and bear it with no true struggle.

Meanwhile the vaporetto was approaching the station and his pain and perplexity grew to the point of distraction. Tormented as he was, he felt it impossible to depart, yet none the less so to turn back. He entered the station racked by indecision. It was very late; he had not a moment to lose if he was to catch the train. He both wished to and did not. But time was pressing, goading him onward, and he hastened to purchase his ticket and then peered through the tumult for the hotel employee on duty there. The man appeared and informed him that the large trunk had been dispatched. Dispatched? Already? Yes, as ordered: to Como. To Como? And after a flurry of comings and goings, irate questions and embarrassed answers, it came out that back in the luggage room of the Hotel Excelsior the trunk had been thrown together with some other people's luggage and routed in a totally misguided direction.

Aschenbach had difficulty maintaining the only plausible facial expression in the circumstances. A reckless joy, an unbelievable glee took almost convulsive hold of his breast. The hotel employee rushed off to do what he could to stop the trunk, but returned, as was to be expected, unsuccessful. Aschenbach accordingly announced that he was unwilling to travel on without his luggage and had decided to go back and wait at the Hôtel des Bains until the article was retrieved. Was the hotel motor launch still at the station? The man assured him it was just outside, and in a torrent of Italian he induced the ticket clerk to take back the ticket Aschenbach had purchased. Then he swore that telegrams would be sent and no effort spared, nothing left undone to ensure that the trunk be recovered as soon as possible. And thus a most unusual thing came to pass: twenty minutes after arriving at the station the traveler found himself on the Grand Canal making his way back to the Lido.

What an oddly improbable, humiliating, comically dreamlike adventure: taking brokenhearted leave of places forever and then, turned round and spirited back by a quirk of fate, seeing them again within the hour! Spray at the prow, tacking with playful agility between gondolas and vaporetti, the swift little vessel raced towards its destination, its sole passenger concealing beneath a mask of resigned indignation the anxious yet high-spirited agitation of a child who has run away from home. From time to time his breast still shook with laughter at the thought of this mishap, which, he said to himself, could not have befallen even the luckiest of men at a more opportune moment There were explanations to give, astonished faces to confront, but then, he said to himself, everything would be fine again, a disaster averted, a grievous error rectified, and everything he thought he had left behind would once more open up before him, his to enjoy for as long as he so desired . . . And was it only the speed of the launch or was there actually, on top of it all, a breeze blowing in from the sea?

The waves beat against the concrete walls of the narrow canal that runs across the island to the Hotel Excelsior. There a motor omnibus stood waiting to take the returning guest straight to the Hôtel des Bains on the road above the rippling sea. The small, mustachioed manager in the frock coat came down the steps to greet him.

He deplored the incident in his soft, wheedling way, calling it extremely awkward for him and the establishment, but unconditionally condoned Aschenbach's decision to await the trunk there. His room had of course been occupied, but another, equally suitable, would be ready immediately. *"Pas de chance, monsieur,"* said the Swiss lift attendant with a smile as they rode up. And thus the fugitive was lodged once more, and in a room all but identical in situation and furnishing.

Exhausted and benumbed by the strange morning's turmoil, he distributed the contents of his bag about the room and settled into a reclining chair at the open window. The sea had turned a pale green, the air seemed thinner and purer, the beach with its boats and cabanas more colorful, though the sky was still gray. Aschenbach gazed out of the window, his hands folded in his lap, pleased to be back, but shaking his head in displeasure at his fickle nature, his ignorance of his own wishes. He sat thus for perhaps an hour in repose and idle reverie. At noon he spotted Tadzio in his striped linen outfit and red bow returning from the sea to the hotel through the beach gate and along the boardwalks. From his lofty vantage point Aschenbach recognized him immediately, even before getting a clear view of him, and was on the point of thinking something like: So you're still here, too, Tadzio. But at that very moment he felt the casual greeting fade and vanish before the truth of his heart, he felt the rapture of his blood, the joy and agony of his soul, and acknowledged to himself that it was Tadzio who had made it so hard for him to leave.

He sat there perfectly still, perfectly invisible on his lofty perch, gazing within himself. His features were keen, his eyebrows high, his lips drawn into a vigilant, inquisitively intelligent smile. Then he raised his head and with both arms, which had been hanging limply over the back of his chair, made a slow, rising, circular motion that brought the hands forward in such a way as to indicate an opening and spreading of the arms. It was a gesture of willingness, welcome, of calm acceptance.

Four

D ay after day now the god with the flaming cheeks soared upward naked, driving his team of four fire-breathing horses through heaven's acres, his yellow ringlets fluttering wild in the gale of the east wind. A silky white sheen overlay the expanse of slow-swelling Pontos. The sand fairly glowed. Beneath the quivering silvery blue of the ether, rust-colored canvas awnings jutted out before each cabana, and mornings were spent on the sharply outlined patch of shade they created. But evenings were lovely as well, the plants in the park exuding their balm, the heavenly bodies dancing their round, the soft sighs of the night-shrouded sea rising up, casting spells on the soul. Evenings like these bore the joyful promise of a new sunny day of loosely ordered leisure and ornamented with countless and closely packed prospects of pleasant encounters.

The guest detained by so obliging a mishap was far from regarding the recovery of his property as grounds for a new departure. For two days he had had to make do without a few necessities and show up for meals in the main dining room in his traveling clothes. When the errant item was finally deposited in his room, he unpacked completely and filled the wardrobes and drawers with his belongings, resolved to remain for an as yet unspecified period and pleased to be able to spend his beach hours in a silk suit and appear again for dinner at his table in proper evening attire.

The soothing regularity of this existence quickly cast a spell over him: he was charmed by the soft, resplendent benignancy of it all. What a place indeed, combining as it did the appeal of a refined southern seaside resort with a strange, wondrous city in intimate proximity! Aschenbach did not care for pleasure. Whenever and wherever he was called upon to let his hair down, take things easy,

enjoy himself, he soon—especially in his younger years—
felt restless and ill at ease and could not wait to return to
his noble travail, the sober sanctuary of his daily routine.
It was the only place that could enchant him, relax his
will, make him happy. There were times when in the
morning, gazing dreamily at the blue of the southern sea
from under the awning of his cabana, or on a halcyon
night, reclining on the cushion of the gondola taking him
home to the Lido from Saint Mark's Square beneath the
vast, starry firmament—the colorful lights, the melliflu-
ous strains of the serenade fading into the distance—he
would recall his house in the mountains, scene of his
summer labors, where clouds drifted low through the
garden, violent storms blew out the evening house lights,
and the ravens, which he fed, soared to the tops of the
spruces. Then he would feel he had indeed been
whisked off to the land of Elysium, to the ends of the
earth, where man is granted a life of ease, where there is
no snow nor yet winter, no tempest, no pouring rain,
but only the cool gentle breath released by Oceanus,
and the days flow past in blissful idleness, effortless, free
of strife, and consecrated solely to the sun and its feasts.

Aschenbach saw much of the boy Tadzio, saw him almost continually, the narrow confines and common activities making it only natural that the beautiful creature should be close to him throughout the day with only brief interruptions. He saw him, met him everywhere: in the downstairs rooms of the hotel, on the refreshing boat rides into town and back, in the splendor of the square itself, and at various odd times and places dependent on the whims of chance. Chiefly, however, and with a most felicitous regularity, it was mornings on the beach that afforded him extended opportunities for the study and reverence of the fair vision. Yes, it was the daily assurance of good fortune, the periodic recurrence of favorable circumstances that so filled him with contentment and joie de vivre, that made the place so precious to him and strung each sunny day so obligingly to the others.

He would rise early—as was his wont when under the unrelenting pressure of his work—and was one of the first on the beach, when the sun was still mild and the sea a dazzling white, still dreaming. He would greet the gate attendant amiably and nod another friendly greeting to

the barefoot graybeard who readied his place for him—
pulled out the brown awning and moved the furniture
out of the cabana—whereupon he settled in. He then had
three or four hours during which the sun climbed to its
zenith and grew to a frightening intensity, during which
the sea turned a deeper and deeper blue, and during
which he could watch Tadzio.

He would see him coming, from the left, along the
shore, see him emerge from between cabanas, or he
might suddenly realize—not without a pleasant shock—
that he had missed his arrival, that he was already there,
already in the blue-and-white bathing costume that was
now his sole beach attire, and that he had resumed his
customary sun-and-sand activities—the charmingly
frivolous, idly bustling existence that with its ambling,
wading, digging, grabbing, lolling, and swimming was
both play and rest—overseen by the women on the platform calling "Tadziu! Tadziu!" to him in their high-
pitched voices, and he would run up to them, gesturing
animatedly, and tell them what he had been doing, show
them what he had found or caught: mussels, sea horses,
jellyfish, crabs that go sideways. Aschenbach understood

not a word of what he said, yet humdrum as it might be it was mellifluent harmony to his ear. Thus the foreignness of the boy's speech transformed it into music, the exuberant sun poured its copious rays over him, and the sea and its sublime depths provided a constant foil and backdrop for his presence.

Soon the observer knew every line and pose of that body so noble, so freely exposed, joyfully welcoming anew each already familiar aspect of his beauty, and his wonderment and delicate sensual delight knew no bounds. Summoned to greet a guest paying his respects to the ladies at the cabana, the boy would run up out of the water—dripping wet perhaps, tossing back his curls—hold out his hand and—one foot planted on the ground, the other on tiptoe—execute a charming twist and turn of the body, gracefully restless, graciously diffident, and obliging from a sense of *noblesse oblige*. He would lie full length with his towel wrapped round his chest, a delicately chiseled arm resting in the sand, a hand cupping the chin, while the boy addressed as Jasiu squatted at his side, playing up to him, and there could be nothing more tantalizing than the smiling eyes and

lips of the chosen one looking up at his inferior, his servant. He would stand at the edge of the sea, alone,
removed from his family, quite near Aschenbach, erect,
his hands clasped behind his neck, slowly rocking on the
balls of his feet, staring out into the blue in reverie,
while little waves rolled up and bathed his toes. The
honey-colored hair fell gracefully in ringlets at the
temples and the back of the neck, the sun glimmered in
the down of the upper spine, the fine delineation of the
ribs and symmetry of the chest stood out through the
torso's scanty cover, the armpits were still as smooth as
a statue's, the hollows of the knees glistened, and their
bluish veins made the body look translucent. What discipline, what precision of thought was conveyed by that
tall, youthfully perfect physique! Yet the austere and
pure will laboring in obscurity to bring the godlike
statue to light—was it not known to him, familiar to
him as an artist? Was it not at work in him when, chis-
eling with sober passion at the marble block of language, he released the slender form he had beheld in
his mind and would present to the world as an effigy
and mirror of spiritual beauty?

Effigy and mirror! His eyes embraced the noble figure standing there at the edge of the blue, and in a rush
of ecstasy he believed that his eyes gazed upon beauty
itself, form as divine thought, the sole and pure perfection that dwells in the mind and whose human likeness
and representation, lithe and lovely, was here displayed
for veneration. This was intoxication, and the aging
artist welcomed it unquestioningly, indeed, avidly. His
mind was in a whirl, his cultural convictions in ferment;
his memory cast up ancient thoughts passed on to him
in his youth though never yet animated by his own fire.
Was it not common knowledge that the sun diverts our
attention from the intellectual to the sensual? It be-
numbs and bewitches both reason and memory such
that the soul in its elation quite forgets its true nature
and clings with rapt delight to the fairest of sun-
drenched objects, nay, only with the aid of the corpo-
real can it ascend to more lofty considerations. Cupid
truly did as mathematicians do when they show concrete images of pure forms to incompetent pupils: he
made the mental visible to us by using the shape and
coloration of human youths and turned them into

memory's tool by adorning them with all the luster of beauty and kindling pain and hope in us at the sight of them.

Such were the thoughts of Aschenbach the enthusiast, such the feelings of which he was capable. And from the surge of the sea and the glow of the sun there emerged a beguiling tableau. It was of the old plane tree not far from the walls of Athens, that place of sacred shade fragrant with chaste-tree blossoms and decorated with votive images and pious offerings in honor of the nymphs and Achelous, a crystal clear brook flowing over smooth pebbles past the foot of the great spreading tree, past crickets fiddling. On the grass, its mild slope propping up their heads, two men lay sheltering from the day's torrid heat: one elderly, one young; one ugly, one beautiful; the wise beside the desirable. And with compliments and witty, wheedling pleasantries Socrates instructed Phaedrus in the nature of longing and virtue. He spoke to him of the intense trepidation the man of feeling experiences when his eye beholds a representation of eternal beauty; he spoke to him of the desires of the base and impious man who cannot acknowledge beauty when he sees its likeness and is incapable of reverence; he spoke of the holy terror that seizes the noble man when a godlike countenance or perfect body appears before him, how he trembles and loses control and can hardly bring himself to look, yet respects it and would even make sacrifices unto it as he might unto a graven image were he not fearful of seeming foolish in the eyes of men. For beauty, my dear Phaedrus, and beauty alone is at once desirable and visible: it is, mark my words, the only form of the spiritual we can receive through our senses and tolerate thereby. Think what would become of us were the godhead or reason and virtue and truth to appear before our eyes! Should we not perish in the flames of love, as did Semele beholding Zeus? Hence beauty is the path the man of feeling takes to the spiritual, though merely the path, dear young Phaedrus, a means and no more ... And then he made his most astute pronouncement, the crafty wooer, namely, that the lover is more divine than the beloved, because the god dwells in the former, not the latter, which is perhaps the most delicate, most derisive thought ever thought by man and the source of all the roguery and deep-seated lust in longing.

Nothing gladdens a writer more than a thought that can become pure feeling and a feeling that can become pure thought. Just such a pulsating thought, just such a precise feeling was then in the possession and service of the solitary traveler: nature trembles with bliss when the mind bows in homage to beauty. He suddenly desired to write. Eros, we are told, loves indolence, and for indolence was he created. But at this point in his crisis the stricken man was aroused to production. The stimulus scarcely mattered. A query, a challenge to make one's views known on a certain major, burning issue of taste and culture had gone out to the intellectual world and caught up with him on his travels. It was something he was familiar with, something he knew from experience, and the desire to make it shine in the light of his words was suddenly irresistible. What is more, he longed to work in Tadzio's presence, to model his writing on the boy's physique, to let his style follow the lines of that body, which he saw as godlike, and bear its beauty to the realm of the intellect, as the eagle had once borne the

Trojan shepherd to the ether. Never had he experienced the pleasure of the word to be sweeter, never had he known with such certitude that Eros is in the word than during those dangerously delightful hours when, seated at his rough table under the awning, in full view of his idol, the music of his voice in his ears, he formulated that little essay—a page and a half of sublime prose based on Tadzio's beauty—the purity, nobility, and quivering emotional tension of which would soon win the admiration of many. It is surely as well that the world knows only a beautiful work itself and not its origins, the conditions under which it comes into being, for if people had knowledge of the sources from which the artist derives his inspiration they would oftentimes be confused and alarmed and thus vitiate the effects the artist had achieved. How strange those hours were! How oddly enervating the effort! How curiously fruitful the intercourse of mind with body! When Aschenbach put away his work and quit the beach, he felt exhausted and, yes, spent, as if his conscience were reproaching him after a debauch.

The following morning he was going down the front

steps, about to leave the hotel, when he spied Tadzio—alone—nearing the beach gate on his way to the sea. The desire, the mere thought of taking the opportunity to make the casual, offhand acquaintance of the beautiful boy who had unknowingly so elated and moved him, to address him and take pleasure in his response and the look in his eyes—nothing could be more natural, more obvious. The boy was ambling slowly—he could easily be overtaken—and Aschenbach merely accelerated his pace. He caught up to him on the boardwalk in back of the cabanas and was on the point of laying his hand on his head or shoulder—a phrase, some friendly words in French on his lips—when he felt his heart hammering wildly, from the quick pace perhaps, and he was so breathless that his voice would have been hoarse and strained had he tried to speak. He paused and struggled to get hold of himself, but suddenly feared he had been walking too long just behind the boy, feared the boy would notice, turn and look at him questioningly, so he had one more go at it, failed, surrendered, and walked past with downcast eyes.

Too late! he thought at that moment. Too late! But

was it too late? The step he had failed to take might well have led to something joyous, untroubled, and good, to a salutary sobriety. But it is more likely that the aging man had no desire for sobriety, that he was too taken with his intoxication. Who can unravel the essence, the stamp of the artistic temperament! Who can grasp the deep, instinctual fusion of discipline and dissipation on which it rests! For the inability to desire salutary sobriety is tantamount to dissipation. Aschenbach was no longer inclined to self-criticism: taste, the state of mind that came with his years, self-respect, maturity, and a late-won simplicity made him reluctant to analyze motives and determine whether the failure to carry out his intention was due to conscience or to laxity and weakness. He was confused: he feared that someone, if only the bathing attendant, had witnessed his haste and his defeat, and very much feared looking ridiculous. Then again, he made fun of himself for his comically exalted fear. "Daunted," he thought, "daunted like a gamecock drooping its wings in battle. This is surely the god who at the sight of something desirable so breaks our spirit, so utterly dashes our sense of pride against the ground . . ." It was enjoyable, waxing thus rhapsodic, and he was far too arrogant to fear an emotion.

He had ceased keeping track of the time he allotted himself for leisure and gave no thought whatever to going home. He had had ample funds transferred here. His sole concern was that the Polish family would leave, but he learned surreptitiously, by inquiring casually of the hotel barber, that their arrival had barely predated his own. The sun was tanning his face and hands, the bracing salt air was making him more susceptible to emotion, and whereas he had been in the habit of applying any fortification afforded him by sleep, nourishment, or nature immediately to his work, he now allowed the daily invigoration coming from sun, leisure, and sea breezes to dissipate in magnanimously improvident euphoria and sentiment.

He slept fitfully, the delightfully uniform days separated by brief, agreeably restless nights. True, he would retire early, because at nine, when Tadzio disappeared from the scene, the day seemed over to him, but at the first hint of dawn he would be awakened by a sweet panic, his heart would recall its adventure, and, finding it impossible to remain in bed, he would rise and, lightly clad against the morning chill, await the sunrise at the open window. This wondrous event would fill his soul, exalted yet from sleep, with great awe. Sky, earth, and sea still lay in the ghostly, glassy pallor of dawn; a fading star still hovered in the insubstantial heights. But a wind would waft in, a sprightly herald from abodes inaccessible to man, to say that Eos was rising from her husband's side, and then came that first sweet blush of the remotest stretches of sky and sea, presaging the Creation's reappearance to the senses. It was the goddess approaching, the seductress of youths, who had carried off Cleitus and Cephalus and, defying the envy of all Olympus, enjoyed the love of the beautiful Orion. At the edge of the world there was a strewing of roses, an ineffably beautiful shining and flowering, there were childlike clouds, transfigured, translucent, floating like attending *amoretti* in the rosy-blue haze, and a crimson radiance fell upon the sea, its rolling waves seeming to drive it forward, and golden spears flashed from below to the heavenly heights, the gleam turning to fire, soundlessly, the glow and heat and blazing flames billowing skyward with godlike potency, as the sacred steeds of her brother rose with grappling hooves over the planet. Illumined by the god's splendor, Aschenbach, alone and awake, would shut his eyes and let his eyelids be kissed by the aura. Emotions from the past, early, delightful dolors of the heart swallowed up by the strict discipline of his life were now reappearing in the strangest of permutations—he recognized them with a perplexed and puzzled smile. He mused, he dreamed, his lips slowly shaping a name, and, still smiling, his face uplifted, his hands folded in his lap, he would doze off again in his armchair.

Not only did the day begin with fiery festivities, however; it remained curiously feverish, metamorphosed by myth. Whence did it come, what was its source, the sudden breath of air that played so gently and tellingly about his temples and ears like an afflatus from on high? Clouds fleecy white dotted the sky like the gods' own flocks out to pasture. A stiffer wind came up, and Poseidon's steeds reared and shot forward; his bulls, too, the bulls of the blue-curled god, bellowed and charged, their horns lowered. Waves gamboled high like frisky goats amidst the rocks on the beach farther off. A world sacredly deformed and imbued with the spirit of Pan surrounded the spellbound observer, and his heart dreamed soothing fables. At times, as the sun sank behind Venice, he would sit on a bench in the park watching Tadzio, clad in white and with a bright-colored sash, play ball on the rolled gravel court, but seeing Hyacinth who, loved by two gods, was doomed to death. He could fairly feel Zephyr's painful envy of his rival, who neglected his oracle, bow, and zither the better to sport with the beautiful youth; he could see the discus, flung out of cruel jealousy, striking the exquisite head; he, too, turned pale as he caught the buckled body, and the flower which sprang from that sweet blood bore the imprint of his undying plaint . . .

There is nothing more curious or delicate than a relationship between people who know each other only by sight, who encounter and observe each other daily—nay, hourly—yet are constrained by convention or personal caprice to keep up the pretense of being strangers, indifferent, avoiding a nod or word. There is a feeling of malaise and overwrought curiosity, the hysteria of an

unsatisfied, unnaturally stifled need for mutual knowledge and communication, and above all a sort of strained
esteem. For a man loves and respects his fellow man
only insofar as he is unable to assess him, and longing is
a product of insufficient knowledge.

Some kind of relationship and acquaintance was
bound to develop between Aschenbach and young Tadzio,
and the older man was thrilled to discover that his interest
and attention did not go wholly unreciprocated. For
example, what induced the beautiful boy, when appearing
on the beach each morning, to shun the boardwalk
behind the cabanas and saunter through the sand in
front of them past Aschenbach's residence—sometimes
coming needlessly close to him, all but grazing his table
or chair—on the way to the family cabana? Was this the
result of the attraction, the fascination of a superior
emotion on a tender and thoughtless object? Aschenbach looked forward daily to Tadzio's entrance and
at times pretended to be busy when it occurred and let
the boy pass seemingly unnoticed. But at other times he
looked up and their eyes would meet. They were both
as grave as could be on such occasions. Nothing in the

cultivated and dignified mien of the older man betrayed any agitation, yet there was a query, a pensive question in Tadzio's eyes, a hesitation in his gait, and he looked down, then sweetly up again, and when he had passed, something in his bearing intimated that only good breeding kept him from looking back.

Once, however, one evening, something different happened. The Polish boy and his sisters together with their governess had failed to come to dinner in the main dining room, as Aschenbach noted with alarm. After the meal, worried about their absence, he was pacing in evening dress and a straw hat in front of the hotel at the foot of the terrace when all at once he spied the nunlike sisters with their companion and, four steps behind them, Tadzio, emerging into the light of the arc lamps. They were obviously on their way from the vaporetto landing, having dined in the city for some reason. It must have been cool on the water: Tadzio was wearing a navy blue pea jacket with gold buttons and a matching cap. Sunshine and sea air did not tan him, and his skin had the same yellowish marble hue as at the outset, but today he looked paler than usual, whether because of the cool air or the bleaching effect of the lamps' lunar light. His symmetrical eyebrows stood out more sharply; his eyes were a deep, dark shade. He was more beautiful than words can convey, and Aschenbach felt acutely, as he had often felt before, that language can only praise physical beauty, not reproduce it.

He was unprepared for the precious apparition: it had come unexpectedly, and he had not had time to put on a calm, dignified expression. Joy, surprise, and admiration may thus have shown openly in his face when his eyes met those of the boy who had disappeared, and at that instant it happened: Tadzio smiled, smiled at him, with an effusive, intimate, charming, unabashed smile, his lips opening slowly. It was the smile of Narcissus bending over the water mirror, the deep, enchanted, protracted smile with which he stretched out his arms to the reflection of his own beauty, an ever so slightly contorted smile—contorted by the hopelessness of his endeavor to kiss the lovely lips of his shadow—and coquettish, inquisitive and mildly pained, beguiled and beguiling.

The recipient of this smile hurried off with it as if it

were a fatal gift. He was so shaken that he felt compelled to flee the light of the terrace and front garden and hastily sought the obscurity of the rear grounds. Oddly indignant and tender admonitions welled up inside him: "You mustn't smile like that! One mustn't smile like that at anyone, do you hear?" He flung himself on a bench, frantically inhaling the plants' nocturnal fragrance. Then, leaning back, arms dangling, overwhelmed and shuddering repeatedly, he whispered the standard formula of longing—impossible here, absurd, perverse, ridiculous and sacred nonetheless, yes, still venerable even here: "I love you!"

Five

During the fourth week of his stay at the Lido, Gustav von Aschenbach observed some peculiar developments taking place in the world around him. First of all, it struck him that even as the season advanced, the number of guests at his hotel was falling rather than rising and, in particular, the use of German around him had so ebbed and waned that the only sounds reaching his ear at meals and on the beach were foreign. Then one day while conversing with the barber, whom he now patronized frequently, he gleaned a rather unsettling piece of news. Having mentioned a German family that had just departed after a short stay, he added in his chatty, unctuous manner, "But you are

staying on, sir. You have no fear of the disease." Aschenbach looked at him. "The disease?" The prattler did not
reply, acted busy, disregarded the question, and when it
was put to him with more urgency he claimed to know
nothing and attempted with embarrassed eloquence to
change the subject.

That was at noon. A few hours later, the dead calm
and burning sun notwithstanding, Aschenbach went into Venice, driven by a mania to follow the Polish boy
and his sisters, whom he had seen set off for the vaporetto landing with their companion. He did not find
his idol at San Marco. However, while taking tea at his
little round wrought-iron table on the shady side of the
square, he suddenly whiffed an unusual aroma in the
air, an aroma he now felt he had been inhaling for days
without being conscious of it, a cloying medicinal smell
redolent of squalor and sores and dubious hygiene. He
sniffed again and after some thought identified it, then
finished his tea and left the square at the end opposite
the basilica. In that cramped space the smell grew
stronger. The street corners were plastered with printed
notices warning the population on behalf of the city

fathers against eating oysters and mussels and using canal water because of certain gastric disorders that were only to be expected given the weather conditions. The euphemistic nature of the ordinance was clear. Groups of people clustered silently on bridges and in squares, the foreigner among them, sniffing and brooding.

He went up to a shopkeeper leaning against the doorway of his arch amidst strings of coral and trinkets of imitation amethyst and asked what he knew about the disagreeable odor. The man looked him up and down with heavy eyes and promptly roused himself. "A precautionary measure, sir!" he answered, gesticulating. "A police injunction one can only condone. The atmosphere is oppressive; the sirocco is bad for the health. In short, you understand. Perhaps they are being overly cautious . . ."

Aschenbach thanked him and went on. On the vaporetto taking him over to the Lido he now caught a smell of germicide.

Back at the hotel, he headed straight for the newspaper table in the lobby and made a survey of what was available. He found nothing in the foreign-language papers. Those in his own language reported rumors, cited fluctuating figures, reproduced official denials, and questioned their veracity. That explained the departure of the German and Austrian element. Nationals of other countries evidently knew nothing, suspected nothing, and were not yet concerned. "Nothing is to be said about it!" thought Aschenbach anxiously, tossing the papers back on the table. "It is to be hushed up!" Yet at the same time his heart swelled with delight over the adventure the outside world was about to embark upon. For passion, like crime, is antithetical to the smooth operation and prosperity of day-to-day existence, and can only welcome every loosening of the fabric of society, every upheaval and disaster in the world, since it can vaguely hope to profit thereby. And so Aschenbach felt a morose satisfaction at the officially concealed goings-on in the dirty alleyways of Venice, that nasty secret which had merged with his own innermost secret and which he, too, was so intent on keeping: he was in love and concerned only that Tadzio might leave, and he realized not without horror that in the event he would not know what to make of his life.

He had not been content of late to leave the possibility of seeing and being near the beautiful boy to chance or daily routine; he had pursued him, tracked him down. On Sundays, for instance, the Poles never came to the beach. Having surmised that they would be attending mass at San Marco, he would hurry there and, entering the golden dusk of the sanctuary from the square's torrid heat, locate the boy he had so missed, his head bowed at worship over a prie-dieu. He would then stand at the back on the cracked mosaic floor amidst a host of people kneeling, murmuring, and crossing themselves, the massive splendor of the oriental temple weighing opulently on his senses. At the front the heavily bedizened priest walked to and fro, officiating and chanting, the incense billowing up and clouding the feeble flames of the altar tapers, and the sweet and stuffy sacrificial odor seemed to mingle with another: the odor of the diseased city. But through the haze and flicker Aschenbach would see the beautiful boy turn his head, seek him out, and sight him.

Then, as the crowd poured through the opened portals into the radiant square teeming with pigeons, the beguiled traveler would lurk in the vestibule, hiding, lying in ambush. He would watch the Poles go out of the church, watch the siblings take ceremonious leave of their mother, who then set off for home in the direction of the Piazzetta. Having ascertained that the boy, his nunlike sisters, and their governess would turn right and proceed through the clock tower gateway into the Merceria, he gave them a head start and then followed them, followed them furtively on their stroll through Venice. He had to stop when they tarried, duck into food stalls and courtyards when they doubled back; he would lose them, pursue them, hot and exhausted, over bridges and along filthy culs-de-sac, and endure moments of mortal shame when seeing them suddenly come towards him in a narrow passageway from which there was no escape. Yet it cannot be said he was suffering: he was drunk in both head and heart, and his steps followed the dictates of the demon whose delight it is to trample human reason and dignity underfoot.

At some point Tadzio and his entourage would take a gondola, and Aschenbach, concealed by a portico or fountain while they boarded, would follow suit once they had put off from shore. He would instruct the oarsman in an urgent undertone to shadow the gondola just rounding the corner, but unobtrusively and at a distance, promising him a handsome gratuity, and he shuddered when the man assured him, in the same tone and with a pander's roguish solicitude, that he would be well served, well and properly.

Thus would he rock and glide along, reclining on soft, black cushions, behind the other black, beaked craft, to which he was chained by his infatuation. At times it disappeared from view and he grew anxious and distressed. But his guide, as if well versed in such commissions, always managed to bring the coveted object back in sight by some clever maneuver—a shortcut or fleet crisscross. The air was still and noxious; the sun burned intensely through the haze, which colored the sky a slate gray. Gurgling water lapped against wood and stone. The gondolier's call—half warning, half greeting—was answered from afar, from the silence of the labyrinth, by some curious accord. Clusters of blossoms—white and purple, redolent of almonds—hung down over crumbling walls from the small gardens overhead. Moorish window frames stood out in the murk. The marble steps of a church descended into the water, where a beggar, in affirmation of his indigence, squatted with his hat out and showed the whites of his eyes as if he were blind. An antique dealer posted outside his lair beckoned the passerby ingratiatingly in the hope of fleecing him. Such was Venice, the wheedling, shady beauty, a city half fairy tale, half tourist trap, in whose foul air the arts had once flourished luxuriantly and which had inspired musicians with undulating, lullingly licentious harmonies. The adventurer felt his eyes drinking in its voluptuousness, his ears being wooed by its melodies; he recalled, too, that the city was diseased and was concealing it out of cupidity, and the look with which he peered out after the gondola floating ahead of him grew more wanton.

Thus the addled traveler could no longer think or care about anything but pursuing unrelentingly the object that had so inflamed him, dreaming of him in his absence, and, as is the lover's wont, speaking tender words to his mere shadow. Loneliness, the foreign environment, and the joy of a belated and profound exhilaration prompted him, persuaded him to indulge without shame or remorse in the most distasteful behavior, as when returning from Venice late one evening he had paused at the beautiful boy's door on the second floor of the hotel and pressed his forehead against the hinge in drunken rapture, unable to tear himself away even at the risk of being discovered and caught.

Yet he still had moments of pause and near lucidity. Where is this taking me? he would think then with alarm. Where is this taking me? Like any man whose natural gifts aroused an aristocratic interest in his ancestry, he habitually called to mind his forebears during his periods of achievement and success, assuring himself of their approval, gratification, and ineluctable esteem. He thought of them again here and now—enmeshed as he was in so illicit an experience, involved in such exotic extravagances of emotion—thought of their imposing fortitude, their upstanding manliness of character and gave a dour smile. What would they say? But what for that matter would they have said about his life as a whole, a life diverging from theirs to the point of degeneracy, lived under the spell of art, a life about which he

himself, in line with the bourgeois disposition of those
forefathers, had made mocking pronouncements as a
young man, yet which basically so resembled their own!
He too had served; he too, like so many of them, had
been soldier and warrior, for art was war, a grueling
struggle that people these days were not up to for long.
A life of self-domination, of "despites," a grim, dogged,
abstemious life he had shaped into the emblem of a frail
heroism for the times—might he not call it manly, might
he not call it brave? Besides, he had the feeling that the
eros which had taken possession of him was in a way sin-
gularly appropriate and suited to such a life. Had it not
been held in particular esteem amongst the bravest of
nations? Indeed, was it not said to have flourished in
their cities as a consequence of bravery? Countless warrior heroes in older times had willingly borne its yoke,
for no action imposed by a god could be deemed humiliating, and actions that might otherwise have been
condemned as signs of cowardice—genuflections, oaths,
importunate supplications, and servile behavior—such
actions were accounted no shame to a lover but rather
earned him praise.

Thus did the man's infatuation determine his way of thinking; thus did he seek to defend himself and preserve his dignity. Yet at the same time he kept paying willful, obstinate attention to the unsavory events in the depths of Venice, the adventure of the outer world that merged darkly with the adventure of his heart and fed his passion with vague, illicit hopes. Obsessed with the need to obtain new and reliable information on the status and progress of the disease, he riffled through the German papers in the cafés, the ones on the hotel newspaper table having disappeared for several days. They were all assertions and retractions: they would report twenty, forty, even a hundred or more deaths and instances of the disease, after which the existence of an epidemic was if not flatly denied then reduced to totally isolated cases introduced from outside. There was also a scattering of admonitions and protests against the dangerous game being played by the Italian authorities. Certainty was out of the question.

And yet the solitary traveler felt he had a special claim on the secret and, though excluded, took a bizarre pleasure in approaching insiders with insidious questions and forcing them, pledged as they were to silence, to tell outright lies. One day at breakfast in the main dining room he confronted the manager, the light-footed little man in the French frock coat who would circulate among the diners, greeting them and ensuring that things were as they should be, and had stopped at Aschenbach's table for a few words. Why is it, the guest asked casually, as if by the by, why in the world have they been disinfecting Venice all this time?

"It is a police precaution," answered the hypocrite, "an official measure designed to forestall any situation injurious to the public health that might arise as a result of the sultry and unseasonably warm weather."

"The police are to be commended," Aschenbach replied, and after a brief exchange of meteorological observations the manager excused himself.

On that very day, in the evening, after dinner, it so happened that a small group of street singers from the city gave a performance in the front garden. The two men and two women stood by the iron post of an arc lamp, lifting their faces, white in the glare, to the large terrace, where the guests sat ready, over coffee and cold drinks, to submit to the exhibition of local color. The hotel staff—lift attendants, waiters, and office clerks—had come out to listen at the doors to the lobby. The Russian family, eager to enjoy everything to the hilt, had had wicker chairs moved down into the garden so as to be closer to the performers and sat there contentedly in a semicircle, their aged slave standing behind them in her turbanlike kerchief.

Mandolin, guitar, accordion, and squeaky fiddle soon came to life under the fingers of the beggar virtuosi. Instrumental pieces alternated with vocal numbers, one of which featured the younger of the women with her harsh rasp of a voice and the tenor's sugary falsetto in a passionate love duet. But the true talent and leader of the ensemble was unequivocally the other man—the one with the guitar and a kind of baritone-buffo character—who, though he had no voice to speak of, was a gifted mime and possessed of remarkable comic energy. He often broke away from the group, his large instrument in tow, and made his way forward, where his highjinks were rewarded with laughter and encouragement. The Russians in their front-row seats took particular pleasure in so much southern vivacity and exhorted him, clapping and cheering, to ever bolder and brasher antics.

Aschenbach sat at the balustrade, occasionally cooling his lips with the mixture of grenadine and soda water sparkling ruby red before him in the glass. His nerves took in the vulgar tootle and soulful melodies with avidity, for passion dulls one's sense of discrimination and yields in all seriousness to charms that sobriety would treat as a joke or reject with indignation. The sight of the prancing jester had twisted his features into a fixed, almost painful grimace. He sat on, indifferent, while inwardly he was thoroughly engrossed: a mere six paces away Tadzio was leaning on the stone parapet.

There he stood in the belted white suit he sometimes donned for dinner, inexorably, innately graceful— his left forearm on the parapet, his feet crossed, his right hand on his hip—looking down at the minstrels with an expression that was not so much a smile as an indication of aloof curiosity, of courteous acknowledgment. From time to time he drew himself up and, puffing out his chest, pulled the white blouse down through the leather belt with an elegant tug of both hands. But there were also times when—as the aging traveler noted triumphantly, his mind reeling, yet terrified as well—he turned his head over his left shoulder—now wavering and cautious, now fast and impetuous, as if to catch him off guard—to the place where his admirer was seated. Aschenbach did not meet Tadzio's eye, because a humiliating anxiety compelled the errant lover to put an apprehensive curb on his glances. The women guarding Tadzio were seated at the rear of the terrace, and things had now reached the point where the lover needed to be concerned about standing out or arousing suspicion. Yes, several times now—on the beach, in the hotel lobby, in the Piazza San Marco—he had noted with a kind of numbness that they called Tadzio back when he came near him, that they were intent on keeping him at a distance, and he could only acknowledge it as a terrible insult which racked his pride in hitherto unknown torment, yet which his conscience could not gainsay.

In the meantime the guitarist had begun a solo to his own accompaniment, a multistanzaed ditty then the rage all over Italy, to which he brought a vivid, dramatic flair, and each time the refrain came round, the rest of the company chimed in with their voices and aggregate instruments. His build frail, his face gaunt and emaciated, a shabby felt hat pushed back over his neck and a shock of red hair gushing out from under the brim, he stood there on the gravel, apart from the others, in a pose of brazen bravado and, still strumming the strings, hurled his quips up to the terrace in a vigorous parlando, the veins bulging in his forehead from the strain. He seemed less the Venetian type than of the race of Neapolitan comedians: half pimp, half performer, brutal and brash, dangerous and entertaining. The lyrics of the song were merely silly, but in his rendition—what with the facial expressions and body movements he used, his suggestive winks, and the way he licked the corners of his mouth lasciviously—they became ambiguous, vaguely obscene. Protruding from the soft collar of his open shirt, which clashed with his otherwise formal attire, was a scrawny neck with a conspicuously large and naked-looking Adam's apple. His pallid snub-nosed face, its beardless features giving no indication of his age, seemed lined with grimaces and vice, and the two furrows stretching defiantly, imperiously, almost savagely between his reddish brows contrasted oddly with the grin on his mobile mouth. What made the solitary traveler focus all his attention on him, however, was the realization that the suspicious character seemed to bring his own suspicious atmosphere with him: each time the refrain recurred, the singer set off on a grotesque march, making faces and waving, his path taking him directly under Aschenbach's seat, and each time he made his round a strong smell of carbolic acid wafted its way up to the terrace from his clothes and body.

Once the ditty was over, he started collecting money. He began with the Russians—who, as all could see, gave willingly—and proceeded up the steps. He was as humble on the terrace as he had been saucy during the performance. Bowing and scraping, he skulked from table to table, a smile of arch servility baring his strong teeth, though the two furrows were still there, intimidating, between the red eyebrows. The guests observed the exotic creature with curiosity and a certain distaste as he took in his livelihood: they tossed coins into his hat with the tips of their fingers, careful not to touch it.

Eliminating the physical distance between performer and genteel audience, pleasurable as it may be, always produces a certain discomfort. He sensed it and groveled his amends. He went up to Aschenbach, he and his odor, which no one else appeared to mind.

"Tell me," said the solitary traveler in an almost mechanical undertone. "Venice is being disinfected. Why?"

"It's the police," the joker answered hoarsely, "the rules, sir. It's the heat and the sirocco. The sirocco is oppressive. It's bad for the health . . ." He spoke as if surprised one could pose such a question, and demonstrated the sirocco's pressure with the flat of his hand.

"So there is no disease in Venice?" Aschenbach asked very softly between his teeth.

The jester's muscular features settled into a grimace of comic helplessness. "Disease? Of what sort? Is the sirocco a disease? Or our police—are they a disease? You must be joking! A disease? How can you say such a thing? A preventative measure, can't you see? A police order to combat the effects of the oppressive weather conditions . . ." And he gesticulated.

"Very well," said Aschenbach, softly and tersely again, quickly dropping an unduly large coin into the hat. He then dismissed the man with his eyes. The man obeyed, grinning and bowing. But no sooner had he reached the steps than two hotel employees pounced upon him and started cross-examining him in whispers, their faces hard against his. He shrugged, reassuring them, swearing he had been discreet. Couldn't they tell? Released, he went back to the garden and, after a brief consultation with his comrades under the arc lamp, stepped forward once more and sang a song of gratitude and farewell.

It was a song the solitary traveler could not recall having heard before, a brash popular number in an unintelligible dialect and with a refrain of laughter blared out at regular intervals by all four. Words and accompaniment both would then cease, giving way to a rhythmic laughter, patterned in its way, yet very natural-sounding, and made to seem especially lifelike by the talent of the soloist. The artistic distance between him and the distinguished guests having now been reestablished, all his impudence returned, and the artificial laughter he shamelessly aimed up at the terrace was a laughter of mockery. Each time he came to the end of the words in a stanza, he seemed to be battling against an uncontrollable urge: he would choke, his voice would falter, he would press his hand to his mouth and hunch his shoulders till at just the proper moment an unbridled laugh would break, burst, bellow out of him and with such verisimilitude that it had a contagious effect on the audience, causing an objectless, self-perpetuating hilarity to take hold on the terrace as well. This seemed only to redouble the singer's exuberance. He bent his knees, slapped his thighs, clutched his sides, he nearly exploded, shrieking now rather than laughing; he pointed to the terrace, as if there were nothing more amusing than the people laughing up there, and before long everyone was laughing, everyone in the garden and on the verandah, including the waiters, lift attendants, and porters in the doorways.

Aschenbach was no longer reclining in his chair; he sat upright as if to ward off an attack or take flight. But the laughter, the hospital odor wafting up to him, and the proximity of the beautiful boy coalesced in a trancelike spell that, indissoluble and inexorable, held his head, his mind in thrall. In the general commotion and confusion he ventured a glance in Tadzio's direction and, as he did so, noticed that when returning the glance the boy was equally grave, as if he were modeling his conduct and facial expression on Aschenbach's and the general mood had no hold upon him because Aschenbach remained aloof from it. There was something at once disarming and overwhelming in this telling, childlike obedience; it was all the elderly man could do to keep from burying his face in his hands. He also had the feeling that Tadzio's tendency to pull himself up and take deep breaths was the sign of a constricted chest. "He is sickly and has probably not long to live," he thought with the objectivity that strangely enough breaks free on occasion from intoxication and longing, and his heart swelled with pure concern and a concomitant profligate satisfaction.

Meanwhile, the Venetians had finished their performance and were making their retreat. They were accompanied by applause, and their leader did not fail to enhance his exit with a few pranks. His low bows and the kisses he blew provoked such laughter that he redoubled his efforts. Even after his comrades were outside, he pretended to have injured himself by running backwards into a lamppost, and staggered to the gate doubled up as if in agony. There at last he tore off the mask of the comic underdog, stood up straight, indeed, sprang lithely to attention, then stuck his tongue out brazenly at the guests on the terrace and slipped off into the darkness.

The guests dispersed and Tadzio had long since abandoned the balustrade, yet to the displeasure of the waiters the solitary traveler sat on at his table with the remainder of the grenadine. Night proceeded; time dissolved. There had been an hourglass in his parents' house many years before, and all at once he could see the fragile yet momentous little device as if it were standing before him. The rust-colored sand would run soundless and fine through the narrow glass neck, and when the upper bulb was nearly empty a small raging whirlpool would form there.

In the afternoon of the very next day the ever obstinate traveler took another step in his investigation of the outside world, and this time with the utmost success: he went into the British travel agency located just off Saint Mark's Square and, after changing some money at the cash desk, assumed the expression of a suspicious foreigner and asked his awkward question of the clerk who had waited on him. The clerk was an Englishman in a tweed suit, still young, with hair parted down the middle, close-set eyes, and that sober trustworthiness so alien to and unusual in the spry and roguish South. "No cause for alarm, sir," he began. "A routine measure, nothing serious. They often issue such orders to forestall the deleterious effects of the heat and the sirocco..." But when his blue eyes met the stranger's weary, somewhat mournful gaze directed at his lips with mild contempt, the Englishman blushed. "That," he went on in a low voice and with a certain animation, "is the official explanation, which one finds it expedient to accept here. But I can tell you that there is more to it than meets the eye." And then in his honest, genial way he told Aschenbach the truth.

For several years now Indian cholera had displayed a growing tendency to spread and migrate. Emanating from the humid marshes of the Ganges Delta, rising with the mephitic exhalations of that lush, uninhabitable, primordial island jungle shunned by man, where tigers crouch in bamboo thickets, the epidemic had long raged with unwonted virulence through Hindustan, then moved eastward to China, westward to Afghanistan and Persia, and, following the main caravan routes, borne its horrors as far as Astrakhan and even Moscow. But while Europe quaked at the thought of the specter invading from there by land, it had been transported by sea in the ships of Syrian merchants and shown up in several Mediterranean ports simultaneously: it had raised its head in Toulon and Málaga, donned its mask repeatedly in Palermo and Naples, and seemed to have taken up permanent residence throughout Calabria and Apulia. The northern part of the peninsula had been spared. Then in mid-May of this year, on one and the same day, the dread vibrios had been discovered in the blackened, wasted corpses of a ship's boy and a grocer woman in Venice. The cases were kept secret. Within a week, however, there were ten of them, then twenty, thirty, and in different districts to boot. A man from a provincial town in Austria, returning home from a few days' holiday in Venice, died with unmistakable symptoms, and the first rumors of an outbreak in the city on the lagoon made their way into the German press. The Venetian authorities issued a statement to the effect that health conditions had never been better, then took the most essential precautions against the disease. But some food must have been contaminated—vegetables, meat, or milk—because, denied or concealed as it was, death ate a path through the narrow streets, and the premature summer heat, which had warmed the water in the canals, was particularly conducive to its spread. The epidemic even seemed to be undergoing a revitalization; the tenacity and fertility of its pathogens appeared to have redoubled. Recovery was rare: eighty out of a hundred of those infected died, and died a horrible death, because the disease would strike with the utmost ferocity, often taking its most dangerous form, the "dry" form, as it was called. In such cases the body was unable to expel the massive amounts of water secreted by the blood vessels, and within a few hours the patient would shrivel up and choke—convulsed and groaning hoarsely—on his own blood, now thick as pitch. He was fortunate if, as occasionally happened, after a slight indisposition he fell into a deep coma, from which he seldom if ever awoke. By early June the isolation wards of the Ospedale Civile had quietly begun to fill up; room in the two orphanages became scarce, and there was an eerily brisk traffic between the quay of the Fondamente Nuove and San Michele, the cemetery island. But fear of the overall damage that would be done—concern over the recently opened art exhibition in the Public Gardens and the tremendous losses with which the hotels, the shops, the entire, multifaceted tourist trade would be threatened in case of panic and loss of confidence—proved stronger in the city than the love of truth and respect for international covenants: it made the authorities stick stubbornly to their policy of secrecy and denial. The chief medical officer of Venice, a man of outstanding merit, had resigned from his post in high dudgeon and been quietly replaced by a more pliable individual. The populace knew all this, and corruption in high places together with the prevailing insecurity and the state of emergency into which death stalking the streets had plunged the city led to a certain degeneracy among the lower classes, the encouragement of dark, antisocial impulses that made itself felt in self-indulgence, debauchery, and growing criminality. There was an unusually high number of drunkards abroad in the evening; vicious bands of rabble were said to make the streets unsafe at night; muggings were not uncommon and even murders, for it had been shown that on two occasions people who had allegedly fallen victim to the epidemic had in fact been done in, poisoned, by their relatives; and prostitution now assumed blatant and dissolute forms hitherto unknown here, at home only in the south of the country and the Orient.

After thus summarizing the main points, the Englishman concluded, "You would do well to leave, and today rather than tomorrow. The imposition of a quarantine is imminent."

"Thank you," said Aschenbach, and left the office.

The square lay in sunless swelter. Unsuspecting foreigners sat in cafés or stood covered with pigeons in front of the church, watching the birds swarm, beat their wings, or push one another out of the way to peck at the grains of maize they held out in the palms of their hands.

Feverish with agitation, triumphant in his possession of the truth, a repulsive taste in his mouth, and fantastic horror in his heart, the solitary traveler paced up and down the flagstones of the magnificent square. He was trying to come up with a decent and purificatory mode of action. After dinner that evening he could go over to the woman in pearls and deliver the speech he was now formulating: "Permit me, Madam, stranger that I am, to give you a piece of advice, a warning withheld from you by self-serving interests. You must leave, leave immediately, with Tadzio and your daughters! Venice is infested." He might then lay a farewell hand on the head of that taunting deity's agent, turn on his heel, and flee the quagmire. Yet at the same time he felt infinitely far from seriously wishing to take such a step. It would lead him back, restore him to himself, but there is nothing so distasteful as being restored to oneself when one is beside oneself. He recalled a white structure adorned with inscriptions glistening in the evening light and beckoning his mind's eye to lose itself in their pellucid mysticism, then the curious figure of the wayfarer who had aroused a youthful longing for travel and strange, faraway places in an aging man, and the thought of returning home, of coming to his senses, sobering up, resuming his drudgery and craft was so abhorrent to him that his face twisted into an expression of physical revulsion. "Nothing is to be said about it!" he whispered wildly. And added, "I shall say nothing." The consciousness of his collusion, his share of guilt intoxicated him as small quantities of wine intoxicate the weary brain. The image of the infested and abandoned city throbbing wildly in his mind kindled hopes unfathomable, beyond reason, and outrageously sweet. What was that serene happiness he had dreamed of a moment before compared with such expectations? What were art and virtue to him given the advantages of chaos? He said nothing and stayed on.

That night he had a terrifying dream—if dream be the word for the physical and mental experience which did indeed befall him with a life of its own and a sensuous immediacy while he was in a deep sleep, yet in which he did not see himself present, moving through space, external to the events, its scene being rather his very soul, and the events breaking in from without, violently crushing his resistance, a deep, spiritual resistance, and, having run their course, leaving his entire being, the culture of a lifetime, devasted, obliterated.

It began with fear, fear and desire and a dire curiosity about what was to come. Night reigned, yet his senses were vigilant, for from afar there approached a din, a racket, a jumble of noise: a rattling, a blaring and muffled thundering, a shrill cheering as well, and a kind of howl in the form of a long-drawn-out *u*—all of it permeated with, overlain by the eerily sweet tones of a deep-cooing, insidiously persistent flute casting its shamelessly tenacious spell on his innermost being. But he knew a word, obscure yet naming what was to come: *"the strangergod."* In the glow of some smoky embers he discerned a mountainous region similar to the one in which his summerhouse was located, and down from the wooded heights, in the spotty light, past tree trunks and mossy boulders, down tumbled whirling men and beasts, a swarm, a raging horde, inundating the slope with bodies, flames, bedlam, a reeling round-dance: women, stumbling over long hide garments hanging free from the waist, shaking tambourines over heads flung back and moaning, brandishing blazing, sparking torches and naked daggers, holding up snakes with flickering tongues by the middle of their bodies, or cupping their breasts in both hands and shrieking; men with horns coming out of their foreheads, fur loincloths, and shaggy torsos, with necks bent and arms and thighs raised, with a pounding of brazen cymbals and the frenzied beating of drums; smooth-skinned youths prodding he-goats with leafy staffs, clutching their horns, letting themselves be dragged along and whooping at each leap. And the elated revelers howled out their call of soft consonants ending in a long-drawn-out *u*—sweet and wild at once, like none heard ever before, here resounding in the air like the belling of a stag, there resumed by a multitude of voices in boisterous triumph—and goading one another on to dance and fling their limbs about they never let it fade. Yet infusing it all, dominating it all, were the deep alluring tones of the flute. Did they not lure him too, much as he resisted the experience, did they not lure him with shameless resolve to the festivities and the enormity of the ultimate sacrifice? Great was his repugnance, great his fear, honorable his intention to defend his domain against the stranger, the enemy of the serene and dignified intellect. But the noise, the howling, intensified many times over by the reverberating mountainside, grew out of control and swelled into raging madness. His mind was muddled by fumes: the goats' pungent stench, the reek of panting bodies, a smell like that of stagnant waters, and another smell, likewise familiar—the smell of sores and rampant disease. His heart throbbed to the drumbeats, his brain reeled, he was seized by wrath, by blindness, by numbing lust, and his soul longed to join in the round-dance of the god. The obscene symbol, gigantic and made of wood, was bared and raised with a roar of their watchword more ferocious than ever. On they raged, mouths foaming, enflaming one another with lascivious gestures and licentious hands, laughing and groaning, thrusting the goads into one another's flesh and licking the blood from their limbs. But the dreamer was now with them, within them: he belonged to the strangergod. Yes, they were now his own self as they hurled themselves upon the animals, lacerating them, slaughtering them, devouring gobbets of steaming flesh, as they dropped to the trampled mossy ground for unbridled coupling, an offering to the god. And his soul savored the debauchery and delirium of doom.

The stricken man awoke from his dream unnerved and shaken, powerless in the demon's thrall. He no longer shunned the curious glances of the people around him: whether he aroused their suspicion was of no concern to him. They were fleeing, were they not, leaving Venice: many of the cabanas were vacant, a number of tables in the dining room unoccupied, and in the city there was scarcely a foreigner to be seen. The truth seemed to have leaked out despite the tenacious solidarity among interested parties in their attempt to ward off panic. But the woman in pearls stayed on with her family either because the rumors had not reached her or because she was too proud and fearless to heed them. Thus Tadzio stayed on, and Aschenbach, in his beleaguered state, occasionally had the feeling that flight and death might eliminate all life standing in his way and leave him alone on this island with the beautiful boy; indeed, when he sat in the morning by the sea, his gaze—heavy, injudicious, and fixed—resting on the object of his desire, or when, as evening fell, he resumed his undignified pursuit through the narrow streets clandestinely haunted by loathsome dying, things monstrous seemed auspicious and the moral code null and void.

Like any lover, he wished to please and dreaded the thought that it might be impossible. He added cheery, youthful touches to his wardrobe, wore jewels, and used scent; he spent long hours several times a day at his toilet, coming to table bedizened, excited, and tense. Gazing at the sweet youth who had won his heart he was sickened by his aging body: the sight of his gray hair, his pinched features filled him with shame and despair. He felt an urge to revitalize himself, restore himself physically, and patronized the hotel barber with increasing frequency.

Draped in the hairdressing gown, leaning back in the chair under the prattler's ministering hands, he peered in dismay at his image in the looking glass.

"Gray," he said, with a grimace.

"Slightly," the fellow replied. "And all for a wee bit of negligence, a disregard for externals, which, understandable though it is in important personages, is not altogether commendable, especially as it is precisely those persons who should rise above such distinctions as 'natural' and 'artificial.' Were the strictures of certain individuals vis-à-vis the cosmetic art extended logically to include the teeth, the result would be more than a bit repellent. After all, we are only as old as we feel in our minds and hearts, and in certain circumstances gray hair can be more of an untruth than the disparaged corrective. A man like you, sir, has every right to his natural hair color. Will you permit me simply to restore to you what is yours?"

"How so?" asked Aschenbach.

The eloquent barber rinsed his client's hair in two kinds of liquid—one clear, the other dark—and it was as black as it had been in his youth, whereupon he set it in soft waves with his curling iron and stepped back to observe the results.

"All that is left to be done," he said, "is to freshen up the face a bit."

And like someone who cannot stop, is never satisfied, he passed with energetic solicitude from one treatment to the next. Aschenbach, reclining comfortably, unable to resist, indeed, full of hope for the outcome, watched his eyebrows arch more distinctly and evenly, his eyes grow longer, their brightness enhanced by a light line beneath the lids, and farther down, where the skin had been brownish and leathery, saw a blush of sparingly applied carmine, saw his lips, anemic only a moment before, swell raspberry-red and the furrows in his cheeks and around his mouth, the wrinkles under his eyes vanish beneath face cream and the glow of youth—he saw, his heart pounding, a young man in his prime. The cosmetician finally proclaimed himself satisfied by thanking him with the abject courtesy characteristic of such people when serving their clients. "A trifling re-adjustment," he said, putting the finishing touches on Aschenbach's appearance. "Now the gentleman need have no qualms about falling in love." The spellbound lover left, agitated and confused, yet as happy as in a dream. His necktie was red, his broad-brimmed straw hat wound round with a gaudy striped ribbon.

A tepid storm wind had come up, and while the rain was light and intermittent the air was humid, thick, and pregnant with noisome fumes. Besieged by fluttering, clattering, whistling noises, feverish under his rouge, Aschenbach had the feeling that an evil breed of wind spirits was carrying on in space, monstrous sea creatures rooting in, gnawing at, befouling the condemned man's victuals. For the salty weather had robbed him of his appetite, nor could he help imagining food to be tainted by infection.

Trailing the beautiful boy one afternoon, Aschenbach penetrated the stricken city's tangled core. His sense of direction having failed him—the alleys, canals, bridges, and tiny squares in the labyrinth were too much alike—he was no longer certain of even the compass points; all he cared about was keeping track of the vision he was so ardently pursuing and, forced by ignominious vigilance to flatten himself against walls and take cover behind the people ahead of him, he was long unaware of the fatigue, the exhaustion that emotion and unremitting tension had wreaked upon his body and mind. Tadzio walked behind his family, usually letting the governess and his nunlike sisters pass ahead of him when the street narrowed and, sauntering along on his own, he would turn his head periodically to glance over his shoulder with his unusual twilight-gray eyes and make certain his admirer was still following him. He would see him and did not betray him. Intoxicated by this knowledge, lured forward by those eyes, tied inextricably to his passion's apron strings, the love-smitten traveler prowled on after his unseemly hope—only to see it slip away from him in the end. The Poles had crossed an arched bridge, the height of the arch concealing them from their pursuer, and by the time he reached its peak they had disappeared from view. He looked for them in three directions—straight ahead and to the left and right, on both sides of the narrow, dirty quay—but in vain. Unnerved and debilitated, he was finally forced to give up the search.

His head was burning, his body sticky with sweat, his neck quivering, and, plagued by an intolerable thirst, he looked round for immediate refreshment of any kind. He bought some fruit at a little greengrocer's shop—strawberries, soft, overripe goods—and ate as he walked. A small deserted square that seemed under a curse opened up before him, and he recognized it: it was there he had formulated his abortive escape plan a few weeks before. He sank down on the steps of the well in the middle of the square, resting his head against its iron rim. All was quiet. There was grass coming up between the cobblestones and litter lying about. Among the weathered buildings of unequal height ringing the square he noticed one resembling a palazzo and having Gothic arch windows with empty space behind them and balconies adorned by lions. There was an apothecary on the ground floor of another, and the smell of carbolic acid wafted over to him on an occasional gust of warm wind.

There he sat, the master, the eminently dignified artist, the author of "A Wretched Figure," who had rejected bohemian excess and the murky depths in a form of exemplary purity, who had renounced all sympathy for the abyss and reprehended the reprehensible, climbed the heights, and, having transcended his erudition and outgrown all irony, accepted the obligations that come with mass approbation, a man whose fame was official, whose name had been made noble, and whose style schoolboys were exhorted to emulate—there he sat, his eyes closed, with only an occasional, rapidly disappearing sidelong glance, scornful and sheepish, slipping out from under them and a few isolated words issuing from his slack, cosmetically embellished lips, the result of the curious dream logic of his half-slumbering brain.

"For beauty, Phaedrus, mark thou well, beauty and beauty alone is at once divine and visible; it is hence the path of the man of the senses, little Phaedrus, the path of the artist to the intellect. But dost thou believe, dear boy, that the man for whom the path to the intellect leads through the senses can ever find wisdom and the true dignity of man? Or dost thou rather believe (I leave it to thee to decide) that it is a perilously alluring path, indeed, a path of sin and delusion that must needs lead one astray? For surely thou knowest that we poets cannot follow the path of beauty lest Eros should join forces with us and take the lead; yes, though heroes we may be after our fashion and chaste warriors, we are as women, for passion is our exultation and our longing must ever be love—such is our bliss and our shame. Now dost thou see that we poets can be neither wise nor dignified? That we must needs go astray, ever be wanton and adventurers of the emotions? The magisterial guise of our style is all falsehood and folly, our fame and prestige a farce, the faith that the public places in us nothing if not ludicrous, and the use of art to educate the nation and its youth a hazardous enterprise that should be outlawed. For how can a man be worthy as an educator if he have a natural, inborn, incorrigible penchant for the abyss? Much as we renounce it and seek dignity, we are drawn to it. Thus do we reject, say, analytical knowledge: knowledge, Phaedrus, lacks dignity and rigor; it is discerning, understanding, forgiving, and wanting in discipline and form; it is in sympathy with the abyss; it *is* the abyss. We do therefore firmly resolve to disavow it and devote ourselves henceforth to beauty alone, which is to say, simplicity, grandeur and a new rigor, a second innocence, and form. But form and innocence, Phaedrus, lead to intoxication and desire; they may even lead a noble man to horrifying crimes of passion that his own beautiful rigor reprehends as infamous; they lead to the abyss; they too lead to the abyss. They lead us poets thither, I tell thee, because we are incapable of taking to the heavens, we are capable only of taking to profligacy.

Now I shall go, Phaedrus, and thou shalt remain. And when thou seest me no more, then thou too shalt go."

Several days thereafter Gustav von Aschenbach left the Hôtel des Bains later in the morning than usual, as he had been feeling indisposed. He was suffering from dizzy spells that were only partly physical: they were accompanied by a precipitously mounting anxiety and feelings of hopelessness and helplessness, though whether those feelings were contingent upon the outside world or his own existence was unclear. He noticed a large assemblage of luggage waiting to be dispatched in the lobby, asked a doorman which guests were departing, and was given the aristocratic Polish name he had secretly expected to hear. He received the news with no change in his sunken features but with that slight lift of the head one uses to show one has registered something one does not need to know, and then asked, "When?"

"After lunch," he was told, and he nodded and went down to the sea.

It was desolate there. Tremulous ripples ran outward over the broad, flat surface separating the beach from the first long sandbar. An autumnal, off-season mood seemed to lie upon the once so colorful and animated, now all but deserted pleasure haunt, its sand no longer kept clean. A camera, apparently abandoned, stood on its tripod at the edge of the water, the black cloth draped over it flapping noisily in the chilly wind.

Tadzio, with the three or four playmates left to him, was moving about on the right in front of the family cabana, and Aschenbach, resting on his chaise longue about midway between the sea and the row of cabanas, a blanket over his knees, was watching him once again. Their play, which went unsupervised, the women being presumably occupied with travel preparations, looked unruly and was getting out of hand. That stocky fellow with the belted linen suit and black, slicked-down hair— the one they addressed as Jasiu—aroused and blinded by a handful of sand thrown in his face, had forced Tadzio into a wrestling match, which ended in the swift defeat of the beautiful yet weaker boy. But now that it was time to part, the underling's deferential sentiments seemed to have turned to brutal cruelty as he sought revenge for his long enslavement, and the victor, far from releasing his victim, knelt on his back and drove his face so relentlessly into the sand that Tadzio, already breathless from the struggle, appeared in danger of suffocating. His efforts at shaking off the burden of his attacker were convulsive and ceased for moments at a time, recurring only as twitches. Horrified, Aschenbach was about to spring to his aid when the ruffian finally let his quarry free. Tadzio, very pale, raised his body halfway and sat motionless for several minutes, leaning on one arm, hair disheveled and eyes darkening. Then he got to his feet and walked slowly off. The boys called out to him, cheerily at first, then anxiously, imploringly; he did not hear. The dark boy, who must have felt immediate remorse at having gone so far, ran after him and tried to make peace. A heave of the shoulder rebuffed him. Tadzio moved on at an angle towards the water. He was barefoot and wearing the striped linen suit with the red bow.

His head bowed, he lingered at the edge of the sea, drawing figures in the wet sand with the tip of one foot, then entered the shallow water, which even at its deepest did not reach his knees, and waded through it at a leisurely pace until gaining the sandbar. There he stood a moment, gazing out into the distance, then turned to the left and began moving slowly along the long, narrow strip of exposed land. Separated from the shore by a broad stretch of water and from his companions by a proud frame of mind, he walked on, a highly aloof and isolated figure, his hair streaming, in the sea, in the wind, before the misty infinitude. Again he paused to gaze into the distance. And all at once, as if driven by a memory, an impulse, he twisted his body at the waist, hand on hip, into a graceful turn and glanced over his shoulder towards the shore. There sat the observer as he had sat before, when those twilight-gray eyes had first glanced back from the threshold and met his. His head, reclining on the back of the chair, had slowly followed the figure moving there in the distance; now it rose as if to meet the eyes again and sank down on his chest, so that the eyes stared up from below while the face displayed the slack, self-absorbed expression of deep slumber. But to him it seemed as if the pale and charming psychagogue out there were smiling at him, beckoning to him, as if, releasing his hand from his hip, he were pointing outward, floating onward into the promising immensity of it all. And, as so often, he set out to follow him.

Minutes passed before people rushed to the aid of the man, who had slumped sideways in his chair. He was carried to his room. And that very day a respectfully stunned world received word of his death.